THE DEVIL DANCES IN DUST

BY LAVINIA LOVE

Sword of Dominic Press

The Devil Dances in Dust.
©Lavinia Love 2025.
Printed by Sword of Dominic Press.
swordofdominic@yahoo.com
https://swordofdominic.wixsite.com/sodp
First Printing, 2025.
ISBN: 979-8-9938928-1-8.

Book cover by Christian Caudill.
Typeset by Jeremy Hausotter.

TABLE OF CONTENTS

ACKNOWLEDGMENTS

First, to my husband, for his incredible support and honest critique. Your commentary on Paul's actions remains the best I ever received.

To the many,many beta readers and friends who encouraged me, particularly Ari, Mikie and Antoinette McDonald. Without you guys this story would not have been completed, much less published.

A special thanks to the wonderful folk at Henderson Publishing and their assistance in making this story possible.

For all of those who participate with Sword of Dominic Press—writers, editors, beta-readers, cover designers and more. I'd like to thank Sam Ingemi and Allen Samuels in particular, for their time, effort and enthusiasm toward my writing and SODP.

And lastly, thanks be to God, who brought all of these amazing people into my life.

THE DEVIL DANCES IN DUST

Chapter I

Death and Taxes

"REMEMBER, you are dust, and to dust you shall return."

That's what Preacher Greenwood had said when Isaiah Hopkins was buried on the twelfth of July, nineteen thirty-three.

All men become dust.

I think that's why I settled, for now, in the small town of Farewell, Texas. The whole place was barren and covered with dust. The very name of the town implies loss. Man's greed had demanded more than what the land could give. Of course, my whispers helped, encouraging them to plow and grow beyond what was good for the earth, until all that was exposed was the loose topsoil. God offered no tears to wet a land in drought.

I kicked my feet in a jig over the earth, causing great storms of dirt to tower up over the fields and prairies. I covered the land in darkness, sending in demons and temptation on the wind. There are a great many things you could hide in such a disaster, various fears and illnesses. Fear is the gateway to so many evil thoughts.

But, this story isn't about *me*. It's about Paul Hopkins, and how at sixteen-years-old he became the man of his family, standing at the foot of his daddy's grave.

Isaiah Hopkins had been shot three miles outside of Farewell. No good samaritans had passed through to bring the man to a doctor. He bled out alone on the side of the road for a grand total of fifty dollars. The sheriff, who hadn't bothered showing up to the funeral, had yet to find the killer.

I have no dominion over life. That has never been my power, and regardless, I would not want to create. I despise creation. No, I can only influence, manipulate, and destroy what has already been made. Death, however, is a much broader domain, though I am not the master of it either. Death is merely my ally. Death is more feared than something as fragile as life. It is much more permanent. And Death comes for all things.

The service didn't last long. Paul dutifully stood by the grave as the small crowd filed by to pay their last respects to his father. His mother, Gertrude, stood a short distance away managing the two younger children, leaving him to handle the pleasantries.

Mr. Kinley, a handsome man with neatly combed hair, shook Paul's hand firmly, with a serious nod and a heavy voice, "Isaiah was a good man. I'm sorry."

"Thank you, sir."

When Mr. Kinley had moved on to offer condolences to Gertrude, his wife, Mrs. Kinley, spoke quietly to Paul, sniffling into a handkerchief. "Your father was well-loved."

"Thank you."

Following behind their mother were twins Bertie and Bart, who shared their parents bronzed Choctaw skin and proud features. They were both dressed in their Sunday best. Bart held out his palm for a handshake, but Bertie didn't hesitate to hug Paul, her eyes damp. "I'm so sorry for your loss."

Paul heard those words over and over again, murmured as people filed past in obligation.

"I'm sorry."

"He didn't deserve to die like that."

"I'm sorry."

"He was a good man."

"I'm sorry."

Paul struggled to figure out why people were apologizing for something they didn't do. An apology implied a person did something wrong against him, and to the best of his knowledge, they hadn't killed his father. If I wanted to, I could use such confusion to breed resentment toward those only trying to help him. But at the moment I was too busy reveling in the grief and awkward social niceties demanded by a funeral. Perhaps later.

Gertrude spoke softly to Anna, Paul's younger sister, and lovingly touched the white wooden grave marker. Anna followed suit, although not understanding why. Little Anna, who was five, had asked just yesterday over breakfast when daddy was coming home. She'd been the apple of Isaiah's eye, and I was eager to see how life would take bites out of her. Little things are not meant to lose so much so young. Such pain makes my work all the easier.

Matthew, at eleven years old, was mature enough to understand. He'd cried incessantly when he had learned their daddy died, until Paul sternly told him that he had to be strong for Mama and Anna. He touched the grave marker once as well.

"Thank you, Preacher," Paul said solemnly as the gravedigger took over, piling dirt on the cheap wooden coffin. "It was a good service."

My favorite pastor, Preacher Greenwood, was a withered and white-haired man, dressed in a sharply tailored suit, adorned with a simple pocket watch. He was the sort of man that always looked to be in a pious state of mind.

"Your father was a good man, son. It's the least I could offer him on his way to the Lord." He softly cleared his throat, and continued, as if almost embarrassed, "I heard your mother has family in Sacramento. You'll be happy there."

Paul in his too-big black suit that had been darned over with his mother's love, clutched his daddy's bowler hat. Though shuffling his feet he raised his chin, "With all due respect sir, I'll be running the farm now."

"Who do you have to help you?"

"Ma, Matthew, and I can manage," Paul answered simply.

The Hopkins family had been too proud to accept any donations other than the pies and casseroles the women of Farewell had sent over. Asking for help working their land was out of the question.

"Our wheat crop is good enough to tide us over this year."

Pride. This too is one of my favorite morsels of humanity.

"Well, if you ever need anything, son, you know where I am," Preacher Greenwood said kindly. "I'll stop by to visit your mother. She's always comforted by the Word."

Paul shook the preacher's hand with a strong grip. "Thank you sir." The boy, much like the Texan sky, hadn't cried in years. "I'll bring around the money for the service sometime next week."

"Take care now, Paul."

The boy donned his bowler hat, nodding a silent goodbye before following his family out of the small cemetery nestled at the bottom of one of Farewell's only hills.

Anna noticed him following and broke away from her mother, running to her brother with an excited squeal. Paul scooped her up in his arms, and settled her on his shoulders, just like their daddy would have done.

***

The Hopkins family lived in a small clapboard house lined with newspaper to cover the bare wood boards. The kitchen was nothing more than a small counter and an iron stove to warm up what little space they had. The cupboards were bare and had been for a while.

When Paul got inside, Gertrude was already wringing out a

fresh wet sheet. He silently took the other half of the cloth, helping his mother hang it over the door to ward off dust particles. The house was quiet, save for the floor creaking with every step. No one was in the mood to talk.

Gertrude was a strong woman, but even her children could see her starting to wilt from the worry and grief of losing her husband. But ever the mother, she smiled at Paul cupping his cheeks carefully with calloused hands, "Change out of those clothes before you grow into them on me. I'll put supper on."

"Yes ma'am."

Paul was more than willing to take off his funeral clothes and move on with his day. The stiff, scratchy fabric of the ill-fitting suit was more than he could handle on top of everything else swirling in his brain. He folded the suit neatly and tucked it away in his trunk after donning his usual overalls. His mother didn't need any extra mess to deal with right now.

As if nothing else had happened that day, Paul went back into the living space, grabbed his father's rifle, and headed out the door to bring the cow in from the pasture out back.

The Hopkins' property was a generous size, with fields bearing thin strains of yellow wheat, and an old barn made from sod that had once been the house when he was younger. There were remnants of a grass pasture in the distance, but no trees to offer shady relief from the hot sun beating down on the land.

On either side of the Hopkins farm were two others, the Johnsons' and the Kinleys'.

Paul was gratified the Kinleys had come to the funeral. It had been expected since they were close family friends, but he was still grateful for the gesture.

He had grown up with Bertie and Bart since they were around the same age, going to school, playing games, and working with them. Before the Kinleys had stopped being able to afford chickens, the families butchered together, and Bertie always complained of having to de-feather the dead birds.

The Johnsons' house and barns, however, now stood abandoned, like a tiny ghost town in the middle of Texas. They had left for California, like many other farmers, desperate for soil and sky that would not betray them. A more peaceful life.

Isaiah had been a peaceful and God-fearing man. I had a hard time tempting and twisting him while he was alive. He was the simple and practical sort of man I hated.

Paul kept walking, his daddy's rifle in his hands. The longer he held the firearm, the more it struck him that it wasn't his father's rifle anymore. It was his now.

He and that rifle were gonna get to know each other real well.

I encouraged this new development and even nudged his mind to wander. The gun carried so many memories of his father, which would only compound the grief on his soul. Paul's thoughts turned to a particular memory of when his daddy had first taken him shooting.

Paul had been eleven, helping clear dishes off the table, when Isaiah had taken the old rifle off the nails where it hung on the wall and called his son over to him.

"Grab your hat, Paul," he'd said.

"Why?"

"Don't ask why, boy. Just get your hat."

Gertrude had taken notice and frowned, wringing her hands in her apron, before opening her mouth to protest, saying something about Paul still being a child.

"Won't be one forever, Gerty," Isaiah said firmly. "I'm not raising up a boy. I'm raising a man."

Isaiah had taken Paul past the wheat field and into the pasture, pausing only to position old bottles and cans on a small makeshift shelf. They stopped about seventy feet from the setup. He got on one knee, his tan weatherbeaten face wrinkling into a serious expression.

"What's a gun, son?"

"A tool," Paul answered.

Isaiah nodded approvingly. "Every man has to know how to use his tools. I already showed you how to use a hammer and scythe, right? A hammer can be used to build a house or pull out nails. A gun is no different. Either it can feed your family or drive someone off your property."

Isaiah handed the rifle over, and although it was heavy and long in Paul's arms, he did his best to handle it carefully, just like his father. The stock was the smoothest wood Paul had ever seen, glistening in the afternoon sunlight. The steel barrel was nicked and scratched, but polished enough to see his blue eyes reflect back at him.

"What's the first rule about handling a gun?" Isaiah asked.

Paul didn't remember. He never liked being put on the spot for such questions.

"You never point the barrel of this gun at something you don't want shot. So be damned sure when you aim this thing, you want what's in front of you full of lead. You can't take back the pull of a trigger. Understand?"

Paul nodded.

"I asked you a question," Isaiah reprimanded sternly.

"Yes sir."

"Alright, now lift it up—extend your arm here. Good, now tuck it in the shoulder just like that. Now—*hey*! Finger off the damn trigger, boy. Not until you're ready."

"Sorry, sir." Paul hastily apologized, moving his index finger to the side of the stock.

"See that brown glass bottle. Line up your shot—keep that barrel level, it's dipping down. Alright, good. Now, see where that notch is, that's where you're aiming."

"I think I got it," Paul's small arms were getting tired, but he kept looking down the barrel as the bottle came into view once again.

Isaiah helped his son adjust the rifle a bit. "Alright, take a breath, and squeeze the trigger, don't pull."

Paul closed his eyes and squeezed the trigger.

BANG!

The barrel bucked backward into Paul's shoulder, and he might've been thrown off his feet if Isaiah hadn't been there to steady him. It hurt, but not enough for Paul to cry out.

The brown bottle was still standing.

"Sorry."

"What are you sorry for? It was your first shot. You'll get better," Isaiah said. Even though the young Paul had missed, there had been a bit of pride in his voice, the kind of pride only given by a father to his son.

Paul did get better. Every other week, his daddy would hand him the rifle, and they'd go out to the field and shoot at bottles. By his twelfth birthday, he could hit the target eight times out of ten. At greater distances too.

"Good shooting, son," Isaiah would say before they would trek home as the sun went down.

His daddy always took a good long while going back, taking in the endless fields of grass and sky. There were no grand hills or magnificent valleys. Just endless earth.

Isaiah was always watching the earth, taking long walks around the property. Every once in a while he would crouch down on his heels, and take a handful of soil, holding it in his fist like a prayer. Paul watched his daddy repeat the ritual through the years, examining the dirt in his hand and letting it fall through his fingers.

One day, walking back from shooting, Paul finally dared to ask, "What are you doing?"

Isaiah dusted off his hands, coming back to reality. "Appreciating the land."

Paul didn't understand, and said so, possessively holding the rifle close to his chest in his adolescent hands.

"Land's the best thing a man can own. Gives you a place to grow what you want, do what you please, and make your own way," Isaiah said seriously, looking deep into Paul's eyes. "Always take pride in your land. You were born on it and fields kept you fed. It's kept you alive, so you respect it. Tend to it. And if you're good to this land, it'll provide for your children too."

It was that lesson Paul took to heart, certainly more so than the shooting lessons. It was good he had those lessons now that Isaiah was gone.

Ginger was grazing in the pasture where she had been left that morning. Something about that simple fact was immensely comforting to Paul. The world was turning on as usual.

Just like his daddy said, this land would provide for them. Paul was already laying out harvest plans. Despite the drought and constant dust storms, their wheat was holding on. Sure, the field might be a bit thin, but it'd support them for the year.

Paul began to believe the words he'd spoken to Preacher Greenwood. His family would manage. Winter would come, and then the rain.

He tied a loose rope around Ginger's neck, guiding the dumb old cow home to the barn. It was almost dark by the time he made it back. With his rifle by his side, he didn't fear the dark, but with the empty Johnson property to his left, the world seemed a bit more lonely.

The Johnsons' had been good neighbors like the Kinleys before they had been forced to leave.

Once upon a time, his family had owned a horse as well, but no longer. They'd sold the mare two years ago to get them through the worst of the drought. So now Ginger slept in the decrepit barn alone, settling into her pile of straw.

Paul locked up the barn and double-checked the gates. When he finally made it back inside the house and hung the rifle up on the hook where it belonged, he found his mother slumped over the table among paper and envelopes, sleeping. Next to her was a plate with a bit of cornmeal mush and hard-boiled eggs.

It pained Paul that his mother was using the last of their precious eggs on a meal when he wasn't even hungry.

He gently shook her shoulder, "Ma . . . Ma, it's getting late.

"Sorry—" Gertrude sat up groggily, rubbing her face in her hands "—must have dozed off. You should get some rest too."

"I will, Ma," Paul promised. He began to gather and shuffle the papers back in order, attempting to help Gertrude the best he could.

"I can clean this up," Gertrude said, trying to wave him off. She had intended to handle this quietly and without fuss while he was outside. She hadn't wanted to burden Paul with the contents of the mail, but he had already noticed.

"Ma, what is this?" Paul took a closer look at the paper. It was a letter from the bank.

As it turned out, after years of dust storms, drought and no crop, Isaiah had taken the loan out to help pay for farm equipment and seed in the stupid hope that this season would be different. Now, that stupid hope was Paul's as he stared at the notice.

They were late on their loan payment.

"Can we afford this?" Paul asked.

"It's just a few bills," Gertrude answered, trying to placate the growing concern in her son. "Nothing to worry about."

"We owe for the funeral—"

"It's a setback. We'll have money coming," Gertrude said, tiredly kissing her son's forehead. "We'll make enough this harvest."

Paul nodded, "The fields look good, but the loan …''

"We buried your daddy today," Gertrude said curtly, her voice on the verge of cracking. There was only so much she could bear. "Whatever we need to talk about can wait until tomorrow."

"Yes, ma'am."

CHAPTER II

SHERIFFS AND STORMS

FAREWELL was a desolate town. Nothing more than a small collection of filthy buildings with peeling paint and rope tied between them, barely a shadow of the lively and welcoming place it used to be. Many local tenants and surrounding farmers had already been evicted, culling the population. Others had chosen to leave of their own free will in the hopes of a better life elsewhere.

With the Prohibition in effect, the town's saloon had been re-dubbed as a "gentlemen's club," but it was an open secret that the proprietor, Mr. Gill, still served alcohol. As the sheriff was a man inclined to drink, he had decided not to do anything so long as Mr. Gill gave him a cut of the profit.

Greed is easy to plant in someone's mind. All you have to do is make them discontent with what they have. There isn't a single person in the world who doesn't want something they're not in possession of.

Paul had never been inside the saloon. Yet, whenever he passed the building, he always took time to glance at the notice board secured to the siding. Seeing if there was anyone looking to buy or sell certain items, or advertisements for local events that provided him a brief moment of escape. Apparently, there was gonna be a dance and picnic held by the church. Such amusement is trivial and pointless in the long term. I can never understand the point of humans giving importance to such detritus, but frivolity and temptation to lust was something I always encouraged.

A few people who recognized Paul offered greetings or condolences for his loss. He nodded in appreciation with a tip of his hat, and continued toward the bank.

See, Paul had a few errands to accomplish on behalf of his mother—and one of his own. He had elected not to tell his mother about his decision to check on their account in the wake of learning of their financial predicament. It would only worry her further.

This is when I began to truly take an *interest* in Paul Hopkins.

Initially, I had just been following in the aftermath of Isaiah's murder: reveling in the sins of the killers and soaking in that delectable grief. Souls are easier to tempt after a tragedy.

But now, here Paul was going behind his mother's back to figure things out of his own volition. His intentions were good; he wanted to help Gertrude. But there are many proverbs about the dangers of good intentions.

In all its glory, the Plains Union Bank was nothing more than a red brick building with a cheery sign painted in deep green and gold. Inside, the wood floors were polished and the service counters freshly dusted. There were even a few benches should they somehow be needed. For the time being they remained empty.

I do love making a place hellish enough no one can think about sparing a moment to take a rest.

"I can help you over here!"

Esther McGraw stood behind the counter, waving Paul forward. He had been sweet on Esther since he was fourteen, having gone to school with her and finding her to be the prettiest thing in the world. Her strawberry-blonde ringlets hung in a bob, framing a heart-shaped face with dimpled cheeks. Her dress was her favorite shade of red: burgundy.

For a moment, Paul hesitated. His nerves always failed him when it came to Esther. Not only that, he wondered if it was more appropriate to call Esther "Miss" or "Ma'am." He had gone to school with her, and he knew her well enough. And she was un-married.

Yet, she was at work and deserved the respect of a bank teller.

Paul removed his hat—his parents had raised him right after all—and approached the counter, "Miss McGraw."

"You know you're allowed to call me Esther," she said with a forced smile, as if she hadn't realized it was Paul she called over. "What can I do for you, Mr. Hopkins?"

"You know you're allowed to call me Paul."

"Not on the clock, I'm afraid," Esther said, taking a deep breath and blinking back a couple of fat tears.

"Why are you crying, Miss?"

The poor boy couldn't help but ask. He was very doglike in that way— always eager to please.

"I'm sorry . . . I was gonna go to his funeral. Your father was a nice man, but . . . I had to work."

"It was a small service," Paul said, offering a kerchief from his pocket. "We uh . . . got your casserole. It was very kind of you, Esther."

Esther wiped her eyes a bit, sniffling. When she was able to finally meet Paul's gaze again, her expression was one of genuine concern.

"How are you doing? How's your mother? And your brother and sister?"

What was he supposed to say? That his mother looked more tired and gray with each passing hour? That Matty almost cried when he left for town, worried Paul wouldn't come back? He couldn't. So, he did what anyone does when asked about per-sonal grief and lied.

"Ma is doing as best as can be expected. So are Matty and Anna. They're smart kids."

"And you?"

"I'm okay, Esther. We're managing," Paul said, changing the subject quickly. "The wheat is looking real good this year."

"Well, if you ever need another casserole or anything, you know where I live," Esther said, absentmindedly smoothing her skirt. "Now, what can I help you with?"

"I'm just here to check on my family's account. We've never been short on the loan before, and I don't intend to start now."

"Let me check the ledger and see what you got," Esther said, pulling a large book from behind the desk, and flipping through it. "Well, it says here you have eight dollars and sixty-four cents left in the account . . . the last payment toward the loan was July first."

"What?"

That wasn't right.

Esther flipped the book around to show him, pointing to the ink neatly printed on the ledger line. "That's the last total we have."

"There must be some mistake," Paul insisted.

"Well, the last withdrawal was . . . '' Esther paused, pursing her lips and taking a single second to collect herself, "the last withdrawal was made by Mr. Hopkins on the eighth of July, for fifty dollars . . . before he went to Worthingtown."

Paul stiffened, the significance of the day still fresh in his mind. Worthingtown was a settlement not too far from Farewell. Isaiah's body had been found on the side of the road halfway between the two towns.

"What was the balance before that?"

"Fifty-eight dollars . . . and sixty-four cents."

"Did he say why he withdrew that much money," Paul asked bewildered. His father had withdrawn almost their entire savings.

Esther shook her head hastily, "No."

"There had to be a reason. Did he say anything else?"

"I'm sorry," Esther said, closing up the ledger. "He didn't say anything when he came to take the money. I thought y'all were leaving town."

"No, we're not leaving town," Paul replied. "Why would you think that?"

Now Esther was the one to tense up, coiled like the rattlesnake I knew her to be.

"Well, your father didn't have enough savings to get the loan at the time . . . so he put down the farm as collateral."

It's incredible what suffering can be wrought because of an abstract concept. Money is only paper when it comes down to it.

It took the dumb boy a few moments to understand what Esther was saying: if they defaulted on the loan, they would lose the farm. Paul ruminated for a moment on his predicament, fighting to keep a straight face.

"Thank you . . . for letting me know."

"Anything else I can help you with," Esther asked.

"Actually," Paul said, glad for the excuse to talk to Esther longer, "Anna needs a new dress, but I figure a lady might have a better idea of what a little girl would like in terms of color."

"Is your ma using cotton or linen?"

Paul blushed in embarrassment. Even though the Hopkins weren't the only family to rely on flour sacks for clothing, they were still proud people who hated to admit it.

Esther didn't seem to notice and beamed in response, "I would love to!"

"Esther!"

Mr. Ned Washburn was one of my favorite people in Farewell who also happened to be the owner of Plains Union Bank. He had a pleasant, personable face that masked the ugly lurking beneath the skin.

His hair was slicked to the side like a lopsided waterfall and he wore a fine pinstripe suit with a velvet vest stretched over his round abdomen. He always had a taste for the finer things.

Ned and I got real acquainted a few years earlier in Osage County. The man had come from nothing, but had a ravenish desire even I hadn't managed to satiate . . . *yet*. Like a moth to flame, he willingly gave in to all manner of sin.

You can plant a seed in a man's mind, but pulling out the weeds of deep-rooted sin in a man's soul . . . well, you need a *Savior* for that kind of gardening. Ned Washburn happily spurned the idea he would ever need one. I won't reveal all the evil deeds he committed, that would be pointless.

Sin is between man and God after all.

Unfortunately, our fun jaunt in Osage County didn't last long. So with his ill-gotten gains, Ned made his way to Farewell and started this bank, leeching off the town's misery. He serves my purposes and in exchange he gets rich in this life, never minding the next.

Ned and I are wonderful friends, even if he doesn't know it.

"McGraw, I need you upstairs. I have some other work for you if you're just standing there," Ned said. Only Esther and I took notice of the cunning malice in his gaze.

"I'm just finishing up with Paul here, Mr. Washburn. I'll be up in a second," Esther said, a nervousness creeping into her voice that she disguised with a smile and subtle bob of her head. The cheerful girl who had existed minutes before had disappeared—a shell of the girl she used to be.

"Mr. Hopkins," Ned corrected sternly.

"Yessir," Esther said, correcting herself.

Ned ignored her comment and turned his attention to Paul, "Forgive me, young man. How can we help you today?"

"Just looking into my family's account," Paul said.

"I see. I heard what happened to your father," Ned said, almost lightly. "It's a terrible shame. I'm very sorry."

"Thank you, sir."

"If you're all finished, I'll need to borrow Ms. McGraw." Ned turned to leave, back straight and smug, as if he'd won a competition the others didn't know they were playing.

"Go with anything pink if you can. All little girls like pink," Esther advised, not forgetting Paul's last request. Her posture had similarly shifted, but rather than inflating herself like her boss, she had somehow managed to make herself smaller.

"I should get back to work."

Twice now, Esther had helped him. Paul nodded his head, donning his hat once more. The poor boy hadn't noticed the subtle change in Esther.

"I'm in your debt, ma'am."

He wouldn't know how much for quite some time.

At the grocers, Paul stayed focused on the essential things his family needed. It was amusing to watch him agonize over every item, and whether or not his family truly, desperately, needed the purchase. Anything the store had was going to be better than the canned tumbleweed leaves and spare bacon grease waiting at home.

He did take Esther's advice and found a small sack of flour that was wrapped in pink flowers for Anna's dress.

Paul would have bought Anna silk if he had been able to pay for it. Quite greedy, if you ask me.

His financial troubles at the store only made his worries weigh on him all the more, but nothing more heavy than his conversation with Esther. They were on the cusp of losing the farm, with no savings to boot. But more importantly, Esther had given him something else: tangible, actionable information to give the boy hope.

There was one person Paul figured might be able to help him, and so he headed to the sheriff's office.

Mortmain Fensky was elected to the position of sheriff a little over eight years ago and, with my help, has held on to the position since. See, Mortmain had been elected during good times, when the land was fertile and people had little to fear or be angry about.

Then, I came to Farewell and encouraged the greed that brought the dust storms. Crops failed, and petty people began to squabble over small matters that escalated into big matters. Crime rose, but there was no rise in support for the law. The town's legal resources were spread thin, leaving an insurmountable stress on the sheriff.

When choosing what particular demon to infect Sheriff Fensky with, I took particular care to gift him with a special oppression. As sheriff, he was an agent of a virtue I despise: Justice. But Justice has no greater enemy than Apathy.

"Sheriff Fensky?" Paul asked, entering the office. It was a clean building with white walls and tiled floors, but other than that the place was in utter disarray. Folders and files were piled on every surface, and chairs for those who might need to wait were shoved into a corner near a small table with a fan. A flag was pinned to the wall near a framed map of Farewell. Fensky was lounging at his desk listening to the radio.

"Can I help you, boy?" Fensky barked, like any good dog of mine.

"Yes, sir. I'm Paul Hopkins, Isaiah's son."

The sheriff sighed, setting aside a tin cup filled with illegal brew, "And what brings you by today?"

"I came to see if you found the man that murdered my father."

"Our investigation is ongoing," Fensky said, a mere repeat of the false promises offered to Gertrude. "These things take time. We don't have a motive, weapon, or any witnesses."

"I do," Paul said.

Sheriff Fensky raised a brow in curiosity. In his mind, the boy was a simple, uneducated hick. An illiterate farmer who had no idea of the law, and the complexities of justice.

"Do enlighten me, boy."

"My father had fifty dollars on him when he was killed. He withdrew the money from the bank the same day he died," Paul explained. "He had it on him, but you never told us there was any money on my father's body."

"I'll take it into consideration."

"The murderer took our entire life savings, sir."

"I told your mother it was probably a robbery gone wrong, and now it's looking like that again. Dozens of gangs might have done it," Sheriff Fensky replied, unconcerned.

"You should look into whoever knew my father withdrew that money or was at the bank with him," Paul said stoutly. "If you find my father's murderer he probably still has the money."

"Quit playing detective, kid," Fensky raised his chin, scoffing. "And if we do, we'll let your *mother* know,"

"You'll let me know," Paul said, puffing up his chest. "I run the farm now, and whatever we find, I'm sure my ma will take it better if it comes from me."

"Yes, I heard you're still running the farm. It's a rather big responsibility for one so young."

"I'm almost seventeen. I ain't that young."

"You are from where I'm standing," Fensky growled, annoyed. "Go home. Take care of your mother and siblings. Let the men handle this."

Paul resented the implication that he wasn't a man. One didn't bear the news his father was murdered and remain a child. He wanted his daddy's killer to hang.

The curtains rustled as a breeze from outside drifted in.

"You're handlin' it?" Paul said heatedly, drawing himself up to full height—six inches shorter than Fensky, "You're sittin' on your ass!"

Sheriff Fensky stepped toward the boy, slapping him hard across the face with a meaty hand. It'd leave a mark, but that wasn't Fensky's concern. His tone was low and dangerous.

"You show me some respect, boy. You're damn lucky I'm looking into this at all. I don't usually care about the corpses of cowards."

The blow had only fueled Paul's anger. He didn't have that deep, sweet rage that melted on my tongue quite yet, but such things take time to simmer and cook. I can satisfy myself with a taste for the time being.

"You call my father a coward again!" Paul stared daggers at the sheriff, undeterred.

Fensky grabbed the front of Paul's shirt, pushing him up against the wall, blowing the smell of sour whiskey over the boy.

"Your daddy was a coward and a piece of shit. He was leaving your ma and siblings alone in the world to fend for themselves, and didn't have the decency to leave y'all the cash."

"Yer lyin'," Paul seethed through gritted teeth, struggling under the grip of the older, stronger man.

"Isaiah knew you'd lose the farm. It was just easier to leave you all behind. I've seen it before," Fensky said, giving Paul one final violent shove against the hard wall before letting go and stepping back. "Your daddy was just the only one dumb enough to get himself shot in the process."

Paul came to his feet, wiping the blood from his mouth, not daring to say another word. His face stung, but not as badly as the blow to his pride.

"You got any more bullshit to spew at me," Sheriff Fenskey threatened, itching for an excuse to beat the boy further.

Paul swallowed, tasting the iron in his blood.

"No sir."

❧ ❦ ❦ ❦ ❦ ❧

Didn't I say evil is easily blown in on the wind of a dust storm? Even so, it bears repeating. The dust and dark hide many wicked things.

Paul wasn't far from home and had a view of the barn, when a looming black shadow rolled over the land, blotting out the sun. A chill gathered in the air and he quickened his pace, clutching the precious grocery bags. He was no stranger to dust storms and knew he only had minutes before it thrust complete darkness upon him. It was deadly getting caught up in such a maelstrom.

However, getting lost was the least of his worries as the wind picked up; Paul still needed to breathe. One can only hold their breath for so long before being forced to inhale the flecks and particles cutting through the air. However, the cost of breathing was high. With each breath he gambled, the higher the chance of contracting pneumonia: a final card dealt from all that dust settling at the bottom of his lungs, slowly choking him to death. It was how a great deal of infants and elderly had met their end.

Paul fought the whole way, bent over against the roaring wind, every step a herculean effort. When he finally reached the barn, he dumbly felt around until he managed to grab hold of the guide rope.

The sand and dirt whipped around him, scratching at his skin and stinging his eyes. Clinging to his lifeline, Paul blindly hauled himself down the rope, like a sailor raising a flag. It was slow progress, but he made it to the house.

The door was locked.

He shouldn't have been surprised as Gertrude in all likelihood did this to prevent the wind from banging the door open and shut without end. Even if there was a chance he might be heard over the storm, Paul had no recourse to screaming either, lest his throat be filled with flying earth. He desperately beat his fist against the door, over and over until the latch lifted, and his ma pulled him inside into her arms.

"Dear Lord above," Gertrude breathed in relief, "I thought you were caught out in it."

"I'm alright, Ma."

Gertrude immediately offered him a wet cloth to keep over his face, which he took gratefully. Her brow furrowed in concern, "What happened to your face?"

"Took a bit of a tumble in the storm," Paul lied sheepishly, holding out the bags of groceries. "But I got everything we needed."

Gertrude sighed, relieving him of his burden before returning to her task of hanging fresh wet sheets over the doors, windows, and walls. A noble effort, but ultimately a futile one. Bits of dust were already sprinkled over the floor and counters. They only had a few more minutes, if that, before the entire world turned as black as pitch.

Then came the screaming, incessant and earsplitting, from the mouth of a terrified five-year-old girl.

"Mama, she won't shut up!" Matty complained from the bedroom doorway.

"Come here and help me wring these sheets out then. Paul can handle Anna," Gertrude replied distractedly.

Paul didn't argue. His mother was tired, and no one wanted to deal with screaming on top of the storm. He entered the bedroom with trepidation and a wet cloth in hand, steeling himself against Anna's shrill shrieks.

She was on the floor throwing an undignified tantrum, kicking violently at Paul as he approached, red-faced and tear-stained. A thin layer of dust had already settled on the bedclothes.

Nimbly avoiding a well aimed kick to his shins, Paul sat as close as he dared.

"Come on, Anna, you got to wear the face cover and keep the dirt out of your mouth." He tried to offer her the wet cloth.

"I don't care!" she yelled.

He looked around, spotting her doll on the bed. He picked it up, then offered it to Anna with the cloth over the doll's face, "Miss Maise wears one."

Defiantly, Anna turned away stubbornly before she started to scream again.

I hate children. Always so loud and disgusting. Their only worthy purpose is to drive those around them to sin.

Paul resisted the urge to throw the stupid toy across the room. He scooted closer, trying to pull her near him. He knew Anna was scared of the dark. And the loud wind. And the way Mama's forehead wrinkled every time a storm came across the horizon.

"Come here."

"No!" She pulled away from him, her whole face damp and snot covered. "I want Daddy!"

Paul exhaled. It should have been obvious. He hadn't considered it, thinking a child couldn't comprehend. But children know more than adults care to admit. Even with a loose grasp on the concept of death, Anna still knew her daddy went somewhere and had never come back.

She was still waiting for him to walk through the door and hold her.

Their world kept getting darker until it blanketed them entirely.

Paul missed his father too. How could he not? In his grief, he locked himself in a room darker and more alone than the one he was in now.

I know that if a person stays deep in the darkness too long, they'll even start to lose sight of themselves.

Little Anna squeezed her eyes shut and finally conceded, clinging to her brother as he helped hold the wet cloth over her face. Paul finally whispered the unsaid truth he had kept buried since learning his father was dead.

"I miss him too, Anna."

He really didn't know what to do without his daddy, and the troubles just kept piling up at his feet.

The wind howled outside like a rabid coyote, rattling the house as violently as prey in the storm's maw. Paul was thankful for it. That it drowned out his words, keeping his weakness secret. He had to be strong, just like he'd told Matty to be.

It's hard to tell the passing of time when there's no sun, but they stayed put well into the next day. The family weathered the storm in silence to limit the inhalation of dust. Anna tired herself out from crying and fell asleep at some point. Gertrude held her close, keeping the girl covered with a damp sheet that Paul morbidly thought looked like a shroud.

Finally, the storm broke and light crept into their lives again.

Gertrude rolled up her sleeves and wielded her broom like a battle-ax throughout the house, attacking all the dirt settled over the floor. She was a firm believer that cleanliness was next to godliness, and would not tolerate a filthy home. She set Anna loose with a small brush to clean off the surfaces, and instructed Matty to take down the protective sheets so they could be rinsed and rehung.

With a grunt of effort, Paul forced the door open, fighting against the drift of earth that had piled up in front of the door.

"I'm gonna check on Ginger."

He needed to get out of the house. To breathe without fear or a wash cloth over his nose. The first inhalation of the crisp morning air hit his lungs like a soothing balm.

That breath quickly abandoned him, leaving his mouth drier than any dust storm could cause.

The yellow grains of wheat were twisted and bent toward the earth in a tangle, as if trampled through by horses from hell. Entire patches of grain had been torn from the soil and scattered on the wind that carried this destruction, and with it any hope of turning a profit this season.

He had really thought that the land would provide for them. Now, the entire crop was gone.

Chapter III

Alcohol and Onomatopoeia

FTER the storm had passed, the other people of Farewell had picked themselves up again, but Paul had many troubles to occupy his mind, and too much free time to dwell on them.

There was no crop to tend, so he spent his time helping around the house and reading the paper. Looking through the wanted ads was the only way he could justify laying about while bills and missed loan payments grew around them like kudzu.

His mother wouldn't approve of him trying to find work and taking the world on his shoulders, which was why Paul had not told her he was looking. At least, not until he was hired. Better to spare his mother the anxiety.

He was the man of the house now. He would take care of things.

"Ma!" Matty yelled from the living space. Paul had half a mind to smack him for being so loud lest he wake Anna. "Preacher comin' to see us!"

Gertrude sounded equally irritated, but she disguised it well, "What?"

"Preacher Greenwood is heading this way. Looks like he's bringing Bertie too," Matty reported importantly.

There was a gentle clamboring of activity, which Paul could only guess was his mother tidying up to receive guests. He couldn't be bothered to get up and help her. He liked Bertie well enough, but he was content to wallow in bed and eavesdrop.

A knock at the door.

"Good morning, Preacher," Gertrude said politely, opening the door. "Morning, Bertie. Would you like some coffee?"

"No thank you," Bertie said.

"No, that's alright. Don't let me keep you from your baking," Preacher Greenwood said, "I'm just here to check in and see how you're doing. I met this lovely young lady along the way, and we decided to come together."

Bertie's kind voice drifted into Paul's room, "Mama and I made an apple pie for y'all."

"That's very sweet, thank you," Gertrude said politely. Paul and I knew she held no ill will toward Bertie or the rest of the Kinleys, but we both noticed there was a terseness buried beneath the nicety in Gertrude's voice indicating an aversion to the pie. The family still didn't want to accept charity. Charity implied pity, and no one likes to be pitied.

"It was your birthday last week, wasn't it Bertie?" Gertrude asked.

"Yes! See this?" There was a brief moment of silence.

"That's a very lovely watch."

"It was Papa's. He gave it to me, saying I was old enough for a family heirloom," Bertie said proudly.

Paul didn't know how Mr. Kinley could keep up his—or his family's—spirits so high, much less manage to provide for them. Paul needed to know these things, but the one who was supposed to teach him was dead.

"Mama and I wanted to be sure you and the boys are doing alright."

"As best as can be, Bertie," Gertrude said.

"Bertie dear," Greenwood intervened, not unkindly. I think he could tell that Gertrude didn't benefit from the girl's bright optimism. "Would you mind giving Mrs. Hopkins and I a moment?"

"Of course, Preacher," Bertie said. Paul heard the door close behind her as she left.

He quietly positioned himself near the bedroom door, intent on listening to the conversation. Through the crack between the door and the wall, he could see Preacher Greenwood, dressed in a sharp suit and brand-new hat. His pocket watch was also new, Paul suspected, or at least professionally polished.

"How have you been?" The preacher asked. "You can be honest."

"We manage," answered Gertrude, returning to her task. She was kneading dough in a special drawer meant to keep out the dust. It was a fruitless effort and all their bread had a bit of grit to it regardless.

I couldn't let them enjoy their food. That would be too indulgent.

"I do worry for you, especially Paul. He's been . . . different," Preacher Greenwood said, taking a seat at the table. "I heard he made trouble for the sheriff in town not too long ago."

"Trouble with the sheriff?" Gertrude balked, "That certainly doesn't sound like Paul . . . ''

"Do you think a boy his age will tell you everything?"

Paul suppressed an indignant huff. He didn't appreciate that the Preacher was speaking about him, and impugning his honor, without him present. But his mother didn't seem to notice, or she didn't care.

"Do you know what happened?" Gertrude asked now standing by the sink.

"Fensky said the boy was belligerent. I don't blame Paul for being upset, and I hate to burden you, but I thought it best if you knew."

Gertrude swallowed hard, the only indication that what Greenwood said bothered her.

"You know I don't care to complain—"

"By all means. I'm sure you have some things to get off your chest," Preacher Greenwood consoled her.

"You saw the fields. We have no way to keep up with the loan." Her voice caught as she continued, "Sometimes I . . . I don't know what to do without Isaiah."

"I can't imagine how hard it is. Do you have family, anyone you can lean on?"

"Geraldine, my sister," Gertrude answered heavily. "But to convince Paul to leave for Sacramento would be twisting a knife in his heart. He's like his father and needs to be his own man, beholden to nobody."

"I see . . . well, I am sorry to hear about your money troubles—"

"I know we can't pay for the funeral right now, but we will—"

"Don't worry about it," Greenwood interrupted Gertrude, irritating Paul. He hated to hear his mother belittled. Still, the coward didn't move from his spot to defend her. "We can figure that all out later."

"Thank you."

"If it's any help, I know the Parsons are looking to buy a cow," Greenwood suggested. "It would take the animal off your hands and provide some money to get you to your sister."

Paul revolted at the idea. Leave?

I knew he wasn't fond of his Aunt Geraldine, who could be a cold and hostile woman. I could only encourage his anger at the idea of being forced to live with her. That same anger was loath to be reconciled with any belief that Preacher Greenwood was trying to help them. Paul couldn't ignore the bad taste left in his mouth. Leaving their home shouldn't need to be an option worth considering.

"I'll consider it," Gertrude said. I didn't know how easy she would be to sway. Her main concern wasn't a lofty ideal like Justice, or Loyalty. She was only worried about whether or not her children would go hungry. Only time would tell.

"Good," Preacher Greenwood said bracingly. "If you need anything, do let me know. I'm here to help."

"We appreciate it, Preacher," Gertrude said.

Paul listened to them talk for a short while longer, each passing second leaving him more angry than the one before. He fumed for nearly thirty minutes trying to wrangle his anger, forcing it down deep inside of him while Preacher Greenwood said his goodbyes.

He tossed aside the old newspaper he had long since stopped pretending to read. The words all blurred together now. Once Paul was sure he wouldn't be stopped, thanks to Anna suddenly demanding Gertrude's attention, he grabbed his coat and headed out the door.

❦ ❦ ❦ ❦ ❦

Farewell is not a forgiving town. Nor is it kind. It can be nice, of course, but not kind. Kindness requires a certain amount of generosity or self-sacrifice, and the people of Farewell were already stretched thin as it was.

After leaving home, Paul went to each of the local farms with a respectful tone and a helpful hand, offering his services in total humiliation. His initial idea had been that many farmers would be grateful for an extra hand come harvest, and he would get some of the profit. Half of the farmers sighed with a shake of their heads and pointed to their own ruined fields.

The other half, the ones who'd managed to hold on to their thin wheat crop, shook their heads with a "no" as Paul held his hat in his hands. Mr. Lantoff didn't even let Paul make his case, simply slamming the door the moment "I'm looking for work" came out of the boy's mouth.

Time and time again he was turned away by neighbors he'd known for years. The same ones who had told him they'd help with *anything* after Isaiah had been murdered.

"We have a mortgage, son," Mr. Eaton said. "We're stretched too thin to hire help."

All empty promises.

So, Paul made the long walk into town, searching for wanted signs. The only one he managed to find was a faded, peeling paper pasted to the inside of the grocer's window.

The bell chimed as Paul entered the shop, and he removed his hat taking in the smell of spices and fresh produce. The shelves were lined with jars and packages of food. He passed by the other customers, using all his willpower to ignore all the things he couldn't afford despite the sharpened ache in his stomach. After seeing his mother fret over their low supply of cornmeal, Paul had skipped breakfast so there would be enough for Matty and Anna.

Mr. Jefferies was at the counter sorting through some of the candy jars he kept near the till. He looked up and saw Paul, smiling for just a moment before it fell to a serious look.

"Paul . . . how are you?"

"Good, you sir?"

"Good, good. What brings you in here?"

Paul gestured to the advertisement, "I saw you was—*were*—hiring out. Thought I'd stop in and see if you still needed the help."

Mr. Jefferies sighed heavily, as if he had been expecting this. "I'm sorry, I should have taken it down. I'm . . . I'm not looking to hire right now."

"Mr. Jefferies—"

"Maybe in Worthingtown—"

"There's gotta be something you need done around here," Paul argued, keeping his voice low so as to not cause a scene. "I don't even need much. Just to hold out until next season."

"Son . . . '' Mr. Jefferies trailed off in an exasperated voice, but he did try to be helpful. "I can't promise anything, but Gill at the gentleman's club said he might be looking for another barkeep."

Alcohol? "My mother—"

"Never has to know. It's the best I can do."

"I . . . ''

Before Paul could wrestle with the internal moral dilemma between accepting employment serving sinful drink or letting his family starve, the bell on the shop door rang once more. Every head turned and voices quieted.

Esther had long grown accustomed to the judgmental stares of the townsfolk and held her head up high as she went about her business, filling her basket without any concern as to the cost.

He was so focused on Esther that it was easy to ignore the people giving her a wide berth, casting dark looks her way as if she were an omen. She was no more than eighteen but that didn't stop me from reminding people what her presence meant and why they hated it. I spare no one, regardless of age.

Esther only took a few minutes to acquire everything she had come for. She didn't acknowledge Paul's presence in the slightest until she approached the counter, gesturing wearily to the till he was standing in front of.

"Do you mind?"

"No, not at all," Paul stepped aside.

"Just hurry up so you can leave," Mr. Jefferies muttered to Esther. "You're making a spectacle of yourself."

Esther's tired voice hardened, and she firmly set her money on the counter, "I'm just picking up groceries, Mr. Jeffries . . . for my family."

"Is there a problem here?" Paul asked.

"No." Mr. Jefferies said shortly, and much to my glee, handing back her change forcefully. Lying *is* a sin

Esther politely picked up her basket and turned on her heel. She brushed past all the others who couldn't take their self-righteous eyes off of her, no matter how subtle they tried to be.

Ever the white knight, Paul followed in her wake. He called after her once he was past the threshold, "Esther!"

She wheeled around with vigor despite looking dog-tired, "Mr. Hopkins, my apologies for my conduct . . . ''

"Mr. Jefferies had no right to be that rude."

"It's nothing," Esther lied again, not that Paul could tell. The poor boy hung on to her every word like it was gospel, "He had an issue at the bank, and he's never gotten over it."

"Everyone else—"

"I know Mr. Jeffries doesn't like me," she hesitated, "Don't worry about this, Paul. Please."

"Do you want to go out some evening," Paul blurted out, for the first time mustering up the courage. "That's all I was gonna ask you—if you wanted to, of course."

"Paul . . . ''

"There's a church dance. I think we should go together if you're willing."

"I appreciate it, I do . . . '' Esther whispered hesitantly, fidgeting with her basket. Neither option was good for her. She truly liked him, but at the moment, even after all she had done, she didn't have it in her to do the merciful thing and say no to his advances.

"I would love to go with you," she said. And there was no lie.

Paul became ecstatic, "Perfect!"

Esther smiled warmly and everything dark that clung to her fell away.

It's shameful how weak I am in the face of Love and Mercy. These virtues are parasites, siphoning away at what wicked havoc I wreak in this world.

"I should be going," Esther said, starting to take her leave, "but I look forward to the dance. I'll see you around, Paul."

Paul was rooted in awe, watching her leave. When he couldn't see her anymore he forced himself to walk dignifiedly into the saloon, rather than skipping to the rhythm of his heart.

❧ ❧ ❧ ❧ ❧

The saloon was dimly lit with smoke wafting about. There were few patrons this time of day, though a pair of gentlemen sat at a corner table with cards and cigarettes. The barkeep approached him with a glass as Paul got closer to the bar, which was lined with empty stools, "What'll you have?"

"Nothing, Mr. Gill," Paul said, "I just heard about the town that you were looking to hire on?"

Paul fought down the wave of fury as Gill gave him the same useless apologetic look every other person kept giving him, "I'm sorry—"

"It's fine," Paul turned back to the door to leave, embarrassed and angry; a half-boiled pot ready to spill over. It was good of me to remind him that a sweet little thing like Esther McGraw couldn't take all his problems away.

"Pour us a round Gill—scotch."

It was the banker, Ned Washburn, who spoke in such a falsely kind way that even I was impressed. He laid down his money and turned his attention to Paul.

"Have a drink with me, son."

"I'm . . . I'm sixteen."

"If you're old enough to work and provide like a man, you're old enough to drink like one." Mr. Washburn clapped a hand on Paul's shoulder, steering him to a table, "Have a seat."

"Sir?" Paul asked, confused, taking a seat at a booth across from Ned. Mr. Gill brought them their drinks and quickly left them alone.

"You're a man now, son," Ned said, lighting a thick cigar. "All business is done over a scotch."

Paul wasn't so sure. He'd never once seen his daddy raise a glass in his life. Isaiah had been a good Methodist and kept his family away from alcohol. However in the hot, dry Texan afternoon, the clink of ice on glass was utterly tempting.

Paul sipped the drink and fought to keep a straight face. Whoever invented alcohol had no accounting for taste.

"So, business?"

Ned nodded, taking a long drag of his cigar. "As your banker, I am acutely aware of your family's financial situation and I wanted to offer my help."

"Help?" Paul asked, the smoke burning his nostrils. He was, as they say, cautiously optimistic.

"I hate to have to turn out a widow with children, especially after what happened to your father. It's not profitable, or good business, but I am willing to offer you a way out of your loan."

Paul became hopeful, the stupid boy he was, "Really? How?"

"I'd like to buy the farm," Ned said. "It's already collateral, but this way your family will be able to settle somewhere comfortable." Paul was dumbfounded. Leave the farm?

"Sir, we don't plan to sell . . . ''

"Son, we both know you don't have the money to cover last month's payment, much less this month. Especially now that you don't have a crop. Either way, the bank will be getting the farm."

"Do you make everybody this offer?"

"I can't save everyone, but I am trying to help your family after your loss," Washburn said incredulously, implying in his tone that Paul was ungrateful. "Ninety dollars to square you away in California, and you don't have to suffer the indignity of being forced out. It's a good deal, son."

"Ninety dollars? The farm has to be worth more than that!"

"Who else is gonna buy it," Ned challenged.

"I'm not sellin'."

"What do you plan to do? Your mother still owes on that loan. Let me do this for you."

Whether or not Ned truly meant it as kindness was none of my concern, but I knew him well enough to know that even his kindness had an agenda. He wouldn't make this offer unless there was something he was getting out of it.

Paul took another drink, burning his throat with the acrid liquid. "My father said to be cautious of men who are suddenly generous. They tend to be makin' up for their guilt."

Ned turned an ugly beet red.

"I thought we could handle this as men."

"Buying me a drink don't—doesn't mean you're entitled to pay us off."

"I'm getting your farm either way, son."

"You can't buy everything with money, Mr. Washburn." Paul downed what remained of his scotch, and slammed the glass down against the table, "Have a nice day."

It's amazing how weightless and elated a person can feel when they act with conviction. Humanity is spineless, so when they do take a stand, it is quite a thing to witness. Of course, that feeling of pride and steadfastness doesn't last long.

Pride comes before the fall, doesn't it?

Paul had a long walk home for Doubt and Fear to creep back and whisper to him, reminding him that he just might've sealed his family's fate. It was a damn shame his daddy wasn't here to teach him, but fatherless or not, Paul was receiving quite the education on the sinful way of the world.

⁂

Paul wrestled with his decision for over a week, agonizing in silence. Explaining Ned's offer to his mother was a moot point; he'd already refused it. If they did lose everything, he couldn't bear it if she knew it was his fault. He could think of a million ways ninety dollars would have helped them.

The easiest way to malcontent someone is keeping them overly occupied with the sorts of things they have no control over. I enjoyed plaguing him with imaginings and scenarios of how he could have handled Ned differently. Violently.

Paul was so preoccupied that even sitting at the table for dinner he hadn't noticed what a dreary and quiet affair mealtimes in the Hopkins home had become. No one talked and instead focused on their tasteless beans and cornmeal mush.

One night after everything was cleaned up, Gertrude sat in her wicker rocking chair, bent over the pink flour sack with a needle in hand, diligently making Anna's new dress. It was methodical the way she stitched the seams together, occasionally snipping or tying the thread. Monotonous as it was, there was a practiced, elegant motion to her stitches.

Anna was next to her for a while, practicing her sewing under her mother's guidance. She was using scraps to make her doll a little pillow. If I had any fondness for children, it might have been cute. I sighed with relief when Gertrude put the brat to bed.

At the table, Paul had taken out the family's battered chess board and was walking Matty through the basics as they played. The younger was learning quickly but had trouble keeping all the pieces straight.

"You can't move a pawn diagonal like that," Paul corrected for the umpteenth time, moving Matty's black pawn back to its starting place.

"You moved it diagonally!" argued Matty, becoming an utterly petulant child crossing his arms.

"Only when capturing pieces, but—" Paul quickly distracted Matty from his ire by suggesting a different move. "—if you move your bishop here, then next round you can take this pawn of mine."

Matty stared at the board, and pointed to the rook, "And this piece can only move in straight lines?"

"Yes."

After a moment of consideration, Matty moved the piece across the board, proudly capturing Paul's queen. No sooner had Matty removed his hand from his piece, Paul moved his knight.

Paul was a defensive player. He was careful in responding to both my and Matty's attacks, retreating and regrouping often. When the game started, he had moved his knight forward, and Matty responded by moving a black pawn forward two spaces. Paul returned the piece back to the starting position like he never moved at all.

"Check," declared Paul. "By taking my queen, you left your king defenseless."

Matty "hmmph'ed" grumpily.

I'll admit I was fascinated by the game, struck by how closely it resembled my work. The world was nothing more than a chessboard between good and evil. Each side moving pieces and attempting to stay three moves ahead of the enemy. All in the hopes of capturing souls rather than pieces.

If we're using chess as a metaphor for life, then Isaiah's death had only been my opening move. Matty's sacrificial pawn, so to speak. Now the game was in motion, and I was playing to win.

Knock Knock.

"I got it Ma."

Paul had no idea who would be here at this time of night, but when he opened the door he was pleasantly surprised to see Esther standing on the porch, wrapped in a thick sweater. He smiled warmly, but she didn't return it, wringing her hands together and avoiding Paul's eyes.

"Hello—Esther?" For a moment, Paul froze in panic, worried he had accidentally stood up the girl of his dreams. He slowly realized this wasn't about the dance that was days away, but rather something far more serious.

"Can I come in?" Esther asked suddenly, as if she didn't force the words out now she would never be able to speak them.

"Who is it, Paul?" Gertrude had already set aside her sewing and stood from her chair.

"Esther."

"Oh come inside dear, and please, have a seat."

Paul stepped back so Esther could pass.

"Thank you," Esther said, taking a seat at the table while Gertrude thought of what refreshment they could offer besides water. No matter how little they had, Gertrude had always impressed on her children the importance of hospitality,

"Paul is teaching me how to play chess," Matty informed Esther as he reset the board.

Gertrude chided, "Matthew, is that how we greet guests?"

"Good evening, Miss Esther," he corrected himself. "Do you know how to play chess?"

"A bit, but I'm not very good at it."

"It's okay. I'm not either."

"He's doing good for someone starting to learn." Paul playfully ruffled Matty's hair, "What brings you over this time of night? Is everything okay?"

Esther's hands returned to her lap, fingers entangled in the skirt of her dress, "No . . . I needed to talk to both of you." There are few things sweeter to me than human misery. The Hopkins were only being polite, but each small act of kindness tortured the girl.

"Esther, what's going on?" Paul asked, resisting every urge that told him to hold her in his arms, to keep her there and tell her everything was going to be alright. She could tell him anything. "It'll be okay."

There was something so innocent about Paul's tone that it broke Esther down to tears, even as she tried to hold them back. At least the girl had the decency to keep her crying quiet, and not wail.

Sin had given the world suffering and people use suffering to justify their sins, trapping them in an unbreakable beautiful cycle. The Hopkins had no clue the suffering she was about to bring into their lives while they tried to console the wretched bitch.

"Esther, sweetie?" Gertrude's motherly instincts took over at the sight of Esther's unbidden tears, placing an arm around her shoulder. She glanced at Paul, "You better put some tea on."

Esther wiped her eyes, "Thank you."

"Something got—*has* you upset," Paul corrected himself.

Esther nodded.

"Matty, go check on Ginger," Gertrude said softly, but firmly, noticing how Esther's eyes shifted nervously to where the child was. Matty obeyed, stopping only to don his shoes before disappearing out the door.

Paul set a kettle of water on the stove and took a seat across from Esther. He didn't dare to sit next to her, but he looked as if he desperately wanted to take her hand and solve all her problems until she laughed again. Even in her pain, he wanted to be nearer to her.

"What happened?"

Esther choked back a sob and shook her head.

Gertrude sighed, gently rubbing the girl's back, "Take your time, dear. It'll come when you're ready."

After taking a few moments to collect herself, Esther gulped down a final sob and took a deep breath, "Mr. Hopkins . . . he came to the bank the day he . . . died."

This perturbed Gertrude, but she maintained her calm demeanor.

"He said he was stopping by the bank, but I didn't think much of it," Gertrude said. Isaiah had always been the one to handle the finances and she had been more than happy to let him. In her opinion those things were better left to the men anyway.

Esther gulped, "He . . . '' She couldn't get the words out before breaking down again.

"Esther," Paul's eye's darkened. "What happened to my father?"

"He was withdrawing money, but he seemed . . . off. I asked if he was alright and he said he was just tired and taking a trip to Worthingtown. While he was putting his money away, I saw he had some papers with him. I didn't think much of it at the time."

"And?"

"I was in Mr. Washburn's office yesterday and I found these." Esther pulled a few documents from her purse and set them on the table.

Upon examination, the first paper was an official-looking document with some big words and legal jargon Paul didn't fully understand, but he got the gist of it. It was a letter from the Mineral and Oil Land Office in Worthingtown, confirming that a land survey would be performed at the Hopkins address. The corners were stained with the unmistakable brown of dried blood.

After a minute, Gertrude silently passed Paul the next paper and his heart settled in his throat. He recognized the handwriting immediately. These were tangible words his father had written, down to the messy signature on the bottom. Paul hungrily read every word like his life depended on it.

> *I, Isaiah Walter Hopkins, give permission for one Edwin Lorry to act on my behalf whenever I am not present in dealings regarding the results of the land survey conducted on my property, May 31st.*
>
> *Should the survey prove that there is oil on my land, I hereby agree to give Edwin Lorry 20% of all incurred profit as compensation for his assistance.*
>
> *— Isaiah Hopkins*

"Ma, did you know about this?" Paul asked. The very idea of oil being on their land ignited his imagination, picturing that liquid gold spilling from tall wells, and the money it would bring. Just like Spindletop.

I let him dream.

"I think this is why Mr. Hopkins died," Esther whispered.

"Why do you say that?" Gertrude asked.

"After Mr. Hopkins left . . . Mr. Washburn asked me where he was going." Esther started to cry again, rubbing her wrists.

Paul tried not to sound betrayed, "You told him?"

"He made me!"

Gertrude sat back weakly in her chair. Paul was too stunned to even move.

It was a difficult thing to wrap their heads around and to grasp that a banker was capable of such cruelty. I had no such delusions.

Esther continued, "The next day I found out Mr. Hopkins had been shot, but no one was talking about missing money. I went to talk to the sheriff and tell him that Mr. Washburn had asked about him, but Fensky told me to keep my mouth shut and that if I talked he'd make sure I'd lose my job, and . . . ''

Her voice was barely a whisper as she trailed off.

Paul swallowed bile. His face was still a bit sore from Sheriff Fensky's blow. He couldn't imagine how the brute had intimidated her.

"How *do* you keep your job, Esther?"

Esther paled. She paused for a long moment, ashamed of her answer. Other than pride, nothing drives people further from repentance than shame.

"Mr. Washburn makes me deliver the eviction notices."

"How—"

"There isn't a thing a hungry mouth won't bite at," Esther snapped, losing all composure. "You don't get to judge me for the things I do to feed my family. We're behind on our mortgage, just like everyone else . . . If I don't do what Mr. Washburn wants, we lose everything."

Like all men who seek power and wealth, Ned is reliant on control. It was a cruel thing to require Esther to deliver ruin to her neighbors. At best, it was cowardly. However, Esther had not been hired for the position because she was the most qualified or experienced, but rather because she was young. Young and so very pretty.

Esther's voice hardened again, "I'd do it again if I have to."

The spectacular thing is I knew she would. Just as I knew how it ate at her heart and soul every time Ned made her deliver a sealed letter under threat of bruises, the smell of cognac on his breath near her ear.

Ned had long since ensnared her into his service. People might not shoot the messenger, but the messenger is still the object of hatred and ire. This was only compounded by the fact that Esther refused to leave her job. After all, who would hire her after she sided with their enemy?

By forcing her to be his harbinger of loss, Ned had turned the town against Esther's presence. Yes, it may be Ned and the bank foreclosing on the people's homes and farms, but she was the face they saw when they received the news.

She would be his undoing before the end.

Paul felt that rare evil temper rise in his chest, but it was toward Mr. Washburn. Not her. Never her.

"Esther . . . where did you find these?"

"After I had spoken with Sheriff Fensky, I found them in Mr. Washburn's office."

Gertrude's brow furrowed, "What were you doing in his office?"

Esther refused to meet Gertrude's eyes, and didn't answer.

It didn't matter to Paul. All he cared was that Mr. Washburn had been in possession of papers that belonged to his daddy—and the sheriff had known about it. There weren't many explanations that would absolve them; none believable.

"Ma, what if he did kill Pa?" Paul asked.

"Then God will see justice done on his soul, on Earth or in Heaven."

Faith. Despite her world falling to pieces and crashing down around her, she still truly believed in her heart that everyone would receive their just reward. It's why I couldn't sway Gertrude entirely, even in her despair.

Despair. It breaks people when other sins can't. After all, hopelessness only exists when there's no inner strength left. Just emptiness. I had spent a good long while emptying Gertrude. All that was left was her faith, her children, and her love for them. I hadn't quite been able to remove those yet.

"It doesn't matter," Gertrude said. "We need to return these to Mr. Washburn's office. No one will learn they're missing and you'll keep your job."

"Ma," Paul said, taking a look at the papers in question, "We might be able to save the farm with these. If we can prove oil is on the land—"

"We don't know that for sure."

"I can head to the office—"

"Your father was shot pursuing this!"

"He wasn't just shot, he was murdered!"

"I know that! He was my husband!" Gertrude yelled louder than Paul had ever heard her, her chest rising and falling with heavy breaths. She wrapped her hands weakly around the edge of the table. "I will not lose my son too."

"The sheriff—" the high whistling of the tea kettle cut Paul off.

He angrily pushed back his chair grumbling, "I got it," and stormed into the kitchen to finish making tea before his mother could stop him. He needed to clear his head.

I wish the poor boy would blow off some steam and lash out, instead of deciding to cool off. I suppose Esther was a good motivator for suppressing his anger.

The revelation that Mr. Washburn killed his father never left Paul's thoughts as he grabbed chipped cups from the cupboard. The pain and helplessness of grief had brewed inside him better than the cheap tea he poured. When he finally sat back down and passed out the beverages, even I might have found him too bitter to taste.

"We have to do something," Paul said.

"The sheriff gets money from Mr. Washburn. He pays off everyone— even me," said Esther numbly. "How else would Mr. Washburn have gotten those papers if not Fensky or whoever killed Mr. Hopkins."

"So what?" Paul insisted. "We can prove he and the sheriff were involved in his death. We can go to Worthingtown—"

"Paul," Gertrude said grimly. "We can't prove anything. It's over."

"These were in his office, Ma!" Paul said, gesturing to the blood-stained documents.

"No. These papers were found in the hands of an eighteen-year-old girl who is often alone in her boss's office. Mr. Washburn will claim Esther felt jilted and is trying to blackmail him. She'll lose her reputation on top of everything else."

"I didn't want—"

"I know," Gertrude interrupted Esther, "but that is how he'll try to spin it."

"I can say I stole them," Paul suggested.

"You can say they fell in your lap, but it doesn't matter as long as Fensky is sheriff," Gertrude replied tiredly. She was beyond grief or fight. "It's best we move on."

Esther was finally able to force herself to sip her tea, "I'm so sorry for my part in this. I didn't know Mr. Hopkins would die."

"Lord knows you suffered enough at Mr. Washburn's hands too," Gertrude said, not unkindly. She gathered up the papers and handed them to Esther. "Make sure these get back to where you found them before Mr. Washburn knows they're missing. You should get home before it's too dark. Paul will walk you."

"He doesn't have to—"

"It's fine." Paul, burning on the fumes of his righteous anger, was eager to leave the suddenly oppressive clapboard house. "Let me get my hat."

Once outside, poor Paul was faced with the sudden realization that he had never been alone with Esther for very long. The silly boy was at a loss for words. He remembered what his ma had taught him and offered his arm. It's the polite thing to do after all. And as stupid as the boy's affections were, I didn't mind it. Esther was just one more thing I could take from him.

"My home is this way," she pointed, accepting his arm.

Almost half a mile later, Paul still hadn't managed to find a single polite topic of conversation.

"I'm sorry about all this," Esther finally said after they had walked a couple hundred feet. Her voice was barely louder than the wind. "I should have said something sooner."

"Better late than never, right?" Paul responded light-heartedly, trying to bring a smile to Esther's face. "And I'm sure it will give Ma some peace having answers."

"I'm sorry I said I'd go to the dance with you." Pretty soon, I'd be able to make Esther apologize for existing. Poor thing *did* bring suffering wherever she went. "It wasn't fair to you."

"What do you mean?"

"I would have liked to go with you, but . . . I understand," Esther trailed off.

"I would still like that, actually," Paul said. "Go dancing, I mean. If you still would like to?"

It was quite infuriating that her involvement in Isaiah's death hadn't created a chasm between them. But *no*, Paul still held a torch for the whore. The boy was fucking dense. Damn him. If I had been able, I'd have slapped him upside the head.

Esther wrapped her sweater around her torso, refusing to meet his eyes. "Paul . . . ''

He reached out and dared to tuck a curl of hair behind her ear, just to be able to see a fraction more of her face. "I mean it."

"Why?"

"Onomatopoeia."

Esther was utterly dumbfounded at his answer, even pausing for a moment on the street before loosening her grip on his arm.

"What?"

"When we were in fourth grade— well you in fifth, there was that spelling bee Ms. Matton made us do, and I . . . I'm still not great with writing and spelling. I lost the first round 'cause I couldn't spell 'dictionary'. Heck, I didn't even know the meaning of a lot of the words that were used. Then it was your turn, and you spelled the word perfectly. Something about it stuck in my head, and I've known that word ever since. Onomatopoeia."

"You remember that?"

"It was the first time I saw you. You were wearing a light green dress and there was a pink ribbon in your hair. One of your shoes was untied."

Esther blushed sheepishly, "My shoe?"

"Yeah. A few months later, Leo sprained his ankle, and you stayed with him and helped him until we got the doctor. The year after, you began sharing lunches with Betty Sue, 'cause her family hit hard times and . . . '' Paul turned equally red and closed his mouth.

They entered the sleeping town, passing buildings lit mostly by the large full moon. Paul preferred it this way. They had the large streets to themselves with no wandering eyes or stares.

Just them.

Esther took his elbow again, and they continued along the

packed dirt path, arm in arm. She considered something before asking, "Have you always been watching me?"

"No ma'am, not like that," Paul replied, hoping he didn't sound perverse, or forward. "It just always struck me what a good soul you were to everyone. Sure, I might have noticed you at the spelling bee, but it was your kindness that kept my head turned—if you don't mind me saying."

Esther was a bit wiser, and more cynical about the world than Paul. She knew herself, and the things she had done to keep her family alive. Given the chance, she'd do them again no matter the cost. Paul wasn't the only one with hungry little siblings in the home.

"I don't think I'm a good person anymore, Paul," she said. It pained her to remember a time when the world had allowed her to be better than she was now.

"I think you just need someone here for you now, like you were there for everyone else."

Esther squeezed his arm just a bit tighter, as if holding on to him was the same as holding on to the idea there was still good in this world.

If I had the power, I would have stripped her of such hope.

The lovestruck fools finally made it to Esther's house.

"This is me," Esther said, pointing at the door awkwardly.

"And . . . here." She slipped the papers into Paul's coat pocket. The only thing of value she could offer him. A sliver of hope that justice might win the day. "Just be careful."

Paul stopped her gently before she walked away. Far too gently than what she was used to.

"I'm glad we got to talk. I can't wait for our dance."

Esther flinched at the sudden gesture but quickly disguised it with a smile. Not the kind of fake smile she wore to protect herself.

The stupid girl was genuine.

"Me too, Mr. Hopkins."

Paul's heart reeled and leapt. "I'll see you around."

"Farewell."

55

CHAPTER IV

COURIERS AND CRUCIFIXES

MATTHEW was sitting at the table, struggling through some math homework his mother had drummed up. Most of the schools had closed down due to all the dust storms, unable to guarantee the students safety. I love an un-educated mind, but Gertrude had forced the child to read and practice arithmetic every day. Today, Paul had been roped into helping Matty with his multiplication tables.

"What's five plus five?"

"Ten," Matty said, clearly not interested.

"Now, add five more."

"Fifteen."

"Ok, so five times two?" Paul asked as he looked over the textbook, trying to find an easier way to explain it. He never really fancied himself a teacher. His mind was a million other places than helping Matty, continually plagued by dark thoughts; utterly distractible. "Sorry . . . five times three."

It was easy enough to connect the dots. Isaiah had taken money from the bank and told Esther. Esther told Mr. Washburn. The papers belonging to Isaiah were found in the banker's office. Paul wasn't particularly clever, but even he could come to the logical conclusion: Mr. Washburn had killed his father, or at the very least was involved.

Esther's revelation had only exacerbated the anger Paul desperately tried to keep buried. Even thinking of Mr. Washburn threatening Esther made his blood boil, which is why every time he closed his eyes I wanted him to imagine what scars she was hiding.

Gertrude had forbidden Paul to speak of what happened. She didn't want to talk about the oil, and she didn't need the little ones traumatized further regarding their daddy's death. She was a simple, levelheaded woman, to whom there was no use in dreaming up money or imagining rescue.

Paul often wondered if his mother even cared at all about what happened. She didn't seem angry, or frustrated, or broken. Sure, she was quieter since Isaiah died and was often lost in thought or prayer. But she kept going in spite of it all, keeping her attention focused on her family and faith.

"Fifteen?" asked Matty.

"Huh?"

"Five times three is fifteen."

"Yeah," Paul said impatiently. Whatever tension was coiling inside of him tightened to the point of almost bursting. "And for five times four?

Matty quickly counted on his fingers, "Twenty?"

"Good job," Gertrude praised, looking up for a moment from her sewing. The fondness for her boys was undeniable. It was disgusting.

Paul suddenly closed the textbook and stood from the table. "Come on, Matty. Let's go for a walk."

"What?"

"It's almost suppertime," Gertrude reminded him, her forehead wrinkling in concern.

"We won't be gone long," Paul assured her, taking the rifle down from the wall. "We'll eat when we get back."

"Paul Jerome Hopkins, where are you taking your brother?"

"He'll need to know how to shoot, Ma," Paul answered, "and it seems I'm the only one able to teach him. I was about his age when I learned."

"Ma, please," Matty begged.

Gertrude pursed her lips like she usually did in the face of something she didn't agree with. Her son had become a bit of an unstoppable force in her life, like the dust storms that plagued them. Something uncontrollable. She knew that if she put her foot down Paul would concede, but the bond between them would be forever damaged if she prevented him from passing on something his father had taught him.

Before she'd know it, both her boys would be men. There wasn't anything in the world that would stop that. Every passing day, Paul reminded her more and more of Isaiah.

Paul wanted to pass on Isaiah's teachings to Matty, but I knew his true motivation. What he really wanted was any semblance of control over his life. It's easy to feel in control with a rifle in your hands and I encouraged that association.

"You'll help him hold it properly," Gertrude instructed firmly. "And have him use a rest for the barrel. Don't stay out too late now."

Paul kissed his mother on the cheek. "Thanks, Ma."

❧ ❧ ❧ ❧ ❧ ❧

Paul handed Matthew the rifle, trying to call to mind everything their daddy had taught him about shooting.

"What's the first rule of using a gun?"

Matty hefted the gun in his arms, "Don't point it at people."

"No," Paul corrected, "you don't point it at stuff you don't want dead. Got it?"

A very lovely distinction, in my opinion.

Matty nodded. Paul wondered if he'd been this small and timid when their father had taught him, barely strong enough to lift the gun to aim.

"See that?" Paul pointed out across the pasture toward a few bottles he had set up on an old crate to act as targets. "Try to hit the one in the middle first."

Matty's face hardened and he nodded, raising the rifle.

"Alright, good. Keep it steady, keep it right there against your shoulder. Now look for your target."

"I think I got it," Matty said, peering down the barrel.

"Just breathe," Paul said, trying to talk him through the process like Isaiah had. "Take your time. We're in no rush."

"What if a guy is running real fast at me?"

"Then you'll want your shot to count," Paul said bluntly.

I am increasingly impressed with the growing crassness of his answers.

"Now, when you're ready, squeeze the trigger . . . Relax, it's your first—"

BANG!

A few hidden blackbirds took flight from the grass, startled by the sudden gunshot.

Matty lowered the gun, squinting toward the target, "Did I hit it?"

"No," Paul said, trying to hide the amusement from his face. He was trying to be supportive and not upset Matty, but even the best of older siblings can feel self-satisfied at their youngers' misfortune, forgetting that they were once young as well.

Matty raised the gun again, taking aim. His arms trembled slightly from the weight of the stock, missing spectacularly when he pulled the trigger. "Damn!"

Paul whacked his brother upside the head, "Don't swear."

Matty shoved the gun back at Paul in retaliation, burning with an unusual fury for a child.

"It doesn't matter!"

The pain in Matty's voice gave Paul pause.

"What doesn't matter?" he asked patiently, carefully taking the rifle from his brother.

"Learning all this, everything," Matty muttered.

"What's gotten into you?"

"I know we might have to go to Sacramento because we lost the crop. I'm not dumb. You and Ma don't gotta keep pretending that everything is okay."

"We don't know if we're moving yet," Paul said, "and you get along great with cousin Reggie."

"I haven't seen him in two years."

"That's not that long ago."

"We're just gonna leave Pa here all alone?" Matty demanded, tears glistening in his little, innocent eyes.

Paul set the gun aside for the time being. In trying to ignore his own grief and tribulations, he'd forgotten Matty had lost his father too.

"He understands why, Matty." Paul lowered himself to a knee, his voice quiet. "Pa isn't gonna be upset if we leave."

"I don't want—"

Paul, to his credit, remained calm and firm in his interruption.

"This isn't about what you want." He sighed deeply and gently placed a hand on Matty's shoulder. "Growing up is about taking care of your family, rather than being taken care of. Understand?"

If people got what they wanted, they'd have their father back. Paul wouldn't have to educate his baby brother about how to take care of the family. Matty would still be at home studying math. Such was the weary way of the world.

"Come on," Paul offered the rifle to Matty, "I don't think you're ready to give up after a couple of tries, are you?"

Matty shook his head, strengthened by his brother's words and example, "No."

"You weren't that far off the first time," Paul encouraged, helping Matthew get into position again.

"Did you hit the bottle the first time?"

"No." It was the truth. It seemed to make Matty feel better, so Paul added, "You just have to practice and be patient."

"Is that what Pa told you?"

"Yes." A lie, but once again it seemed to comfort Matty. These kinda of lies are my favorite— the ones that seem so innocent. After all, who wouldn't tell a little white lie to lift someone's spirits?

Matty took aim with renewed confidence, his finger twitching at the trigger.

"Take your time."

Not five seconds had passed before another gunshot rang out. Paul automatically scolded his brother, "Too soon!"

"I didn't!" Matty protested.

Paul didn't argue back, his paranoia heightening. The gunshot had come a distance from the east, the best he could tell. His first thought was that maybe someone was hunting.

I knew what it was. Soon he would too. Finally, the dumb boy landed on the right answer.

The Kinleys.

"Give me the gun," Paul ordered. He pulled back on the bolt, readying the rifle with another bullet, "Stay close to me, alright?"

"What's going on?" Matty asked, sweet, sweet fear creeping into his voice.

"That gunshot came from the Kinleys' farm," Paul breathed. He couldn't imagine Bart would be out hunting that close to his house. Given what had happened to his Pa, he didn't want to take any chances.

"Just stay close."

Matty obeyed the order, but couldn't stop himself from questioning it, "Why—"

"Mrs. Kinley and Bertie might be in the house alone. I'm just gonna make sure they're alright," Paul said calmly, already trekking through the field. He didn't want to scare Matty. "It's probably nothing, but I'd want Mr. Kinley checking in on Ma and Anna if he thought something was off."

The Kinleys didn't live too far off from where they were in the field. There was no more than three hundred meters of weeds and dead grass between them and the edge of the property. Soon they could see the farmhouse and hear the screams that followed shortly after.

Paul broke into a desperate run. The scream didn't sound quite like Bertie, but he wasn't sure Bart was capable of such a noise. Or what would compel Mrs. Kinley to make the sounds that followed—awful gut-wrenching cries.

Mrs. Kinley was holding Bart just a few yards away from the barn, the both of them sobbing in each other's arms and barely keeping each other on their feet. Paul had never seen anyone so inconsolable.

"Please, Lord, no . . . Lord NO!" She wailed.

Bertie was unmoved, staring inside the barn with blank eyes. She was wringing her hands in her cornflower print dress. Paul would never forget that.

When tragedy strikes, it's always the details people fixate on and remember: patterns on a dress; the creaking of metal chains chiming in the light wind; the smell of hay in the barn; and Mr. Kinley's slack, open jaw as he lay dead on the ground, the pistol spilling from his loose grasp.

No, Paul would never forget that either.

"Stay back!" Paul yelled, throwing out his free hand to halt his brother. Matty didn't need to see this. Personally, *I* think he would have found it interesting.

"Paul—"

"I said back!" Paul ordered, slinging the rifle across his back, then looked to Bart for support. His friend had calmed himself enough to get his mother back to the house, as far away from the gruesome scene as he could manage.

Paul leapt at the chance to send his brother away, "Matty, help Bart with Mrs. Kinley."

Matty obeyed without a word.

"He seemed so happy last night," Bertie whispered, still staring at her father's corpse. The poor girl had been the one to find her father, brains and blood scattered on the dirt and hay.

Her confusion was amusing. If I had been able, I might have given her all the answers. Told her how when the eviction notice came Mr. Kinley fell into hopelessness. How I whispered to him, goading him for his inability to protect his family; reminding him how he couldn't provide. I would have relished the chance to tell Bertie that each day Mr. Kinley put on a mask to hide the fact he was sinking into despair. Then, I would blame her for not noticing.

Despair is a wondrous ally. It's the most effective tool I have for urging someone to take their own life— the gravest of all sins.

Paul gently put an arm around Bertie, coaxing her toward the house, "Let's go inside. You . . . you don't have to see this."

"Should we . . . cover him first," Bertie asked, still too shocked to know what to do.

"Yeah, we'll cover him up."

Paul searched inside the barn for a moment. He found a clean, rough woven horse blanket and spread it over Mr. Kinley. His hand brushed against the corpse's skin, and he couldn't help but notice how still death was. He reached for Bertie, finding himself desperate to touch something that was alive and breathing.

Bertie nodded, numbly holding onto Paul as he murmured soft encouragements to keep her moving toward the porch. Once inside, she immediately went to her mother, resting her head in her lap, and wept.

Mrs. Kinley could only stroke her daughter's hair, kissing her forehead and whisper empty consolations, "Your father loved you, sweetie. He loved you so much."

Then why did he leave them? Paul thought bitterly. He dare not say it out loud. Not in front of people he considered family.

Instead, he simply asked, "Why?"

Mrs. Kinley pursed her lips, still stunned from it all, "We lost the home three days ago."

Paul swallowed, "I'm sorry. We didn't know . . . ''

"Of course not. We didn't say anything," Mrs. Kinley fell silent then continued to comfort Bertie.

They spent the next thirty or so minutes sipping on what was more akin to hot water than proper tea. None of them actually desired anything to drink. It was just a worthless ritual to fill the new void in their lives with something while they tried to comprehend it.

Bart stood suddenly and looked up with red eyes at Paul, tired and weary, but driven by duty. There was no plea or complaint in his voice, "Will you help me?"

"I can get Preacher—" Paul began, understanding his meaning.

"No." Bart decided. "I think it's best if people think he died naturally."

The sweetest part of suicide was the stigma. Humans are averse to pain and the pain of others, but even more so averse to shame. Any perceived stain on their honor stung worse than a hornet.

Bart's concern wasn't out of respect for his father, but by lying he hoped to spare his mother and sister the scandal.

Paul didn't disagree with Bart. He quickly downed his tea, giving instructions to Matty, "I'll come get you in a bit. Help them if they need anything, alright?"

Both boys steeled themselves for the grim work to come. Bart showed Paul where the shovels were in the barn. While Paul would have given anything not to see Mr. Kinley's covered corpse again, he was too loyal a friend to leave Bart alone in this.

They hiked out a distance away from the house, searching for a suitable location. Bart selected a spot underneath a lone tree, up on a small hill overlooking the fields. It was as good a place as any, in my opinion. A corpse has no preference for its burial place.

They got to work digging, and before long their necks were slick with sweat. The earth was hard and unforgiving. Every time Paul split the soil with his shovel, it was another twist in his heart. Bart didn't say anything, keeping his eyes on his task.

Finally, when a shallow grave had been dug, they returned to the barn. Paul hitched up the horses and then helped heft Mr. Kinley into the cart, leaving him wrapped in his makeshift shroud. Bart went back inside, and after a few moments emerged with Mrs. Kinley and Bertie, who was carrying a small package. They processed slowly to the grave site to the sounds of crickets and creaking wheels as the sun set on the day.

"Matty?" Paul asked quietly.

Mrs. Kinley smiled wryly, "I sent him on home. He didn't need to be here for this."

"Thank you."

"Of course, dear." She seemed distracted, but the kindness in her voice indicated deep appreciation that Paul had not left Bart to handle his father's remains on his own.

They arrived at the grave, keeping a somber— yet stoic— demeanor. Perhaps they thought if they cried or raged they would break beyond repair. Without ceremony, the boys maneuvered the corpse out of the wagon. With a couple of ropes they lowered Mr. Kinley's body into the hole in a somewhat dignified manner.

Bart opened the package Bertie had brought, revealing a revolting metal crucifix—a family heirloom of some sort — and nailed it to the tree as a marker. He stepped back after, crossing himself in that vile Christian manner, fighting back tears. His family did the same, Bertie managing to find the strength to recite a psalm I will not repeat. Paul had no words to offer.

Mrs. Kinley tossed a few wildflowers onto her husband's body, "We'll speak to Father Calloway . . . and rebury him proper. I hate to see him stay here."

"We will, Ma," Bart assured her, giving his sister one last hug. "But right now we have to make sure he's covered, alright? Bertie will take you home."

Bertie took her mother's arm, leading her mother away from the grave, "Come on, Ma. We'll let them finish up."

The boys returned to their shoveling, consigning Mr. Kinley to the ground as dusk fell.

Paul now knew why the only thing people managed to say was "I'm sorry" at a funeral. What else did one say at a time like this? But it wasn't what Bart needed to hear right now.

Paul knew what it was like to lose a father and what that does to a growing boy. Bart had become the man of the house, just like he had. Neither of them could afford the luxury of pity or sorrow.

"Do you know what you're gonna do?"

Bart shrugged, "There's a couple of places we might go. I'm old enough to find work somewhere, hopefully."

"Be sure to write."

"Where to?" Bart asked seriously, finally bothering to look away from the grave. "The bank will come for you too."

"So we do nothing? What if I could go after the people that did this?" Paul asked in a low voice.

"Go after Mr. Washburn? Might as well walk into the sheriff's office so he can give you another black eye." Bart said severely, a sharp edge creeping into his voice. I love the smell of fear. The whole farm, and town, stank of it. "That it?"

"That's not—"

"I have to think about my mother and Bertie. Maybe you should think about your family, Paul."

Paul bit his sharp tongue. He *was* thinking about his family. He wouldn't even be in this situation if he hadn't been thinking about justice for his Pa and the wellbeing of his mama and siblings.

But Bart didn't have the fire Paul did. He was a tired, lukewarm soul who burned out burying his idiot father. Paul could see it just as I did.

"You're right. We need to take care of family," Paul said.

Bart's shoulders dropped and he exhaled. All he wanted was the stupid reassurance that he would not relive this. At least not anytime soon. "I'll give you a couple of addresses so you can write. I don't wanna lose touch."

"Me either." Paul hugged Bart one last time. "I'll be sure to write."

Now would be a good time to wax poetic, but I won't. There's always a calm before the storm, so I'll allow them the reprieve of burying their dead.

❧ ❧ ❧ ❧ ❧

Esther knocked on the Hopkins' door four days later.

Paul was playing chess again. Without a field or cattle and no school to attend, the boy was wasting away with boredom. There was nothing else to do when he wasn't helping Gertrude around the house, except perhaps read.

It was Gertrude Paul was playing against now, and he was struggling to keep himself out of check. She was a far more formidable opponent than Matty, quickly eliminating his pieces efficiently with her queen. He only had pawns and a bishop left in play.

"Check," Gertrude said, moving her rook into position.

Paul looked at the board in disbelief, trying to trace his moves as to where he went wrong, "How on earth . . . when I took your pawn, right?"

"You were too focused on protecting your king, you didn't pay attention to anything that wasn't an immediate threat," Gertrude said. "Keep an eye on the pieces I'm favoring."

Yes, Gertrude Hopkins had always been very good at playing the game, hadn't she? It's always troubling for me when a good player teaches others how to win. It means I only have a short time to end the game.

Knock, Knock.

"I got it!" Matty said glad for an excuse to set aside his schoolwork, and hurriedly went to answer the door.

Paul looked down at the chess board, considering his moves. Against Matty, his defensive style was quite effective, but Gertrude had a talent for trapping pieces he left too stationary. He moved his bishop back from its advance, returning it to his side of the board to protect his king from Gertrude's rook.

"You're as good at chess as Pa was," Paul said, but quickly shut up. Speaking about Isaiah was still a taboo topic in the house. It upset Matty and Anna would get her hopes up that their daddy would walk through the door any moment.

But Gertrude smiled slyly, ruefully pondering over past memories. "Who do you think taught him how to play?"

"Really?"

"I did." Gertrude said, and moved her pawn forward a square. "But he always preferred cribbage."

"Esther, why are you crying?"

Paul immediately abandoned the game upon hearing Matty's concerned voice at the door, with no regard to Gertrude, who blinked confusedly. He left the table and flew to the door.

Damn his soul, he really thought himself a white knight, off to save the damsel with wet eyes and pretty curls. He was a lovesick sixteen-year-old boy, of course there was nothing he wouldn't do to make the world right for her.

Esther stood in the doorway, pulling her sweater sleeves down over the purple splotches on her wrists, and blinked a few times. The poor girl couldn't even look at Paul.

"Who hurt you?"

She shook her head at the question, swallowing hard as she handed Paul a single letter sealed in an envelope. It was from the bank.

Paul's heart stopped, "Esther, tell me this isn't . . . ''

She nodded slowly.

Paul's heart sank to his heels and his knees buckled. If he hadn't already been laying a hand on Matty's shoulder, he might have collapsed altogether.

I listened intently as Esther forced out the words, "I'm sorry," but I knew she wasn't. Angry? Regretful? Torn? Absolutely. The girl would never have put Paul through this if she had the choice. I also knew she'd be here tomorrow if ordered.

But Paul didn't know that. He only knew his family was going to end up as broken and homeless as the Kinleys.

Mr. Kinley.

A very horrible thought crossed Paul's mind. "Esther, did you deliver the Kinleys' eviction notice too?"

Esther sniffled and nodded. "I never thought . . . ''

That Mr. Kinley would kill himself? Paul finished mentally. Of course, she hadn't meant it. She only delivered bad news because she was forced.

"Who told you he was dead?" Paul asked.

"Mr. Washburn . . . after the Kinleys filed for bankruptcy," she said, digging her fingernails into her sleeves.

Paul whispered softly, "You shouldn't have had to do that."

Esther broke, pressing her body into Paul's and holding fast for dear life, sobbing into his shoulder.

"I thought you would hate me," she choked.

The fiery rage burning up Paul's heart wasn't ignited by Esther. She wasn't who he was truly mad at. Nevertheless, the fire burned and consumed him.

"It's okay," Paul held her all the tighter, "I could never hate you, Miss McGraw."

It was a soft tone he used, one that would be comforting to the girl, but I could hear the anger in his voice. The righteous indignation toward how Esther had been used.

"Paul?" Gertrude joined them at the door, the familiar crease in her brow deepening. "Esther?"

She didn't even open the envelope as Paul handed it to her, but she gently squeezed his shoulder and blinked back tears. There were no words for this. Not when suffering continued to drain everything from Gertrude's life.

"We knew this was coming," Paul said. But just because you expect the blow doesn't mean it doesn't hurt. "How long do we have?"

Esther sniffled and detached herself from Paul, "He's giving you three days."

"That's all?"

"Well, we'll have to send a telegram to Geraldine today and buy train tickets," Gertrude said, mentally making a list of everything that would have to be done, "but I think we'll manage."

"I'm sorry. I tried to say no . . . ''

"Don't do that to yourself," Paul comforted, taking Esther's hand. A bittersweet resignation clung to his voice, "We knew it would be you."

Esther pulled away and wiped her face once more and composed herself, smoothing her skirt. "The sheriff said I only had ten minutes . . . ''

Gertrude's eyes rested on the fingerlike bruises on Esther's wrists, "No, you'd best be going back to work."

Esther nodded and bravely said her goodbyes before returning to the belly of the beast. Her eyes lingered on Paul, heartbroken and guilty, but also perhaps with a bit of relief. If she couldn't get away from Ned Washburn, at least he could.

If Paul was her white knight, he'd have drawn his sword and charged into battle for her. He'd keep her safe from all the evil things I sent on the wind. But he wasn't a white knight. He was just a boy standing in the doorway, cursing every step that carried her away.

Gertrude smiled bravely for her son before pulling Paul into a hug upon seeing his forlorn expression.

"You've been so strong." She kissed his forehead and brushed away the single tear that fell from his wet eyes, "You don't need to be anymore. We're gonna be just fine."

Paul buried his face in his mother's shoulder.

CHAPTER V

FAITH AND FALLS

HEN there is nowhere left to go, when a man truly hits rock bottom, that is when he either finds God—or he finds me.

The little white Methodist church sat just on the edge of town, as if God had been an afterthought in the town's conception. It was a plain and unspecial building, signified only by the cross affixed to the roof. The inside was similarly lackluster, with plain wood pews facing a pulpit with a Bible, and no one but the wind to keep a sinner company.

Paul removed his hat and took a seat near the front, staring at the Bible but not daring to read. What he desired was wicked, and he would find nothing in the Word but condemnation for such things.

He did offer a prayer. Prayers are useless to me and I have no concern whether or not they get answered. More often than not, they are just whiny pleas for help. I prefer to feed off the emotions that fuel prayers. Desperation. Greed. Grief.

I am not even sure if humans know how to pray simply out of love for God.

Paul leaned back in the pew, sitting in the silence, finally alone with his thoughts and grief. You leave a man alone with grief for too long and wandering wicked ideas begin to settle.

Like any good chess game, his options were countless, but knowing human nature the longer Paul sat there deliberating, the more likely he would trap himself into some dichotomy. This or that. Us or them. Right or wrong.

He could concede the match and move on with a new game. Boring in my opinion, but I can admit it would be the safer option for him.

Or, Paul could rally his pieces and take the board until the king gave up his crown. A risky choice, but a far more satisfying one. One where at the very least he would be remembered as a martyr, instead of dying forgotten by the world.

The silence broke by the creak of the door, the rustle of wind, and approaching footsteps. Preacher Greenwood sat beside Paul, nodding as if coming to some wise conclusion. "I knew you'd come here eventually. Most come looking for guidance and meaning after a violent death like your father's."

"My father is dust now."

Greenwood replied in turn, "You are dust, and to dust you shall return."

"Yeah, and then these damn winds blow us away like everything else," Paul said, growing bitter. "Wasn't God's creation supposed to be good? Or does He just have it out for me?"

"Paul, death is the natural way of the world now. Isaiah's death was not to spite or punish you," Greenwood said.

Paul wasn't here for a sermon. "Mr. Washburn killed my father."

"Now, why would you say that?" Greenwood had the decency to act surprised.

"My father had papers on him when he died, about there being oil on the land. Either Mr. Washburn killed my father, or the sheriff gave them those papers."

"Paul, to what end—"

"To get my family's land," Paul interrupted heatedly. "If there's oil, it's as good as a gold mine. Mr. Washburn has those papers and there isn't a damn thing I can do about it."

"God's will is mysterious. Perhaps you'll find happiness and purpose in Sacramento," Preacher Greenwood suggested.

"I weren't—*wasn't* born in Sacramento. This is where I was raised. That is my family's farm. It was my grandpa's before it passed to my father, and now it's mine and my mother's," Paul snapped. "Mr. Washburn knew that my father thought there was oil on the land. He either killed my Pa or paid off the sheriff to give over those papers."

"How do you know these papers exist?" Greenwood asked, twisting his body toward Paul, as if the boy had finally piqued his curiosity.

"I can't tell you that."

"Lying—"

"I'm not lying, Preacher," Paul said. "I can't tell you."

"Do you have the papers?"

Paul didn't answer.

"Stealing is a sin, Paul," Preacher Greenwood said gravely.

"My family is gonna lose their home," Paul said with pathetic desperation. It was music to my ears. "It might take a miracle to stop that, and there ain't a thing I won't do to make that miracle happen."

"Miracles aren't forced, and they certainly don't come from the hand of man."

"No, but I can make him pay and suffer for what he did to us—what he's doing to all of us."

"Is that really—"

"I could kill him."

It wasn't until Paul said it out loud that he dawned on him that murder was more than just an option for him, but something he *wanted*. It was also the sanest course of action; nothing else would stop Mr. Washburn.

"This is a place of worship, Paul," Greenwood said sharply, seemingly scandalized by the very idea. "God does not take kindly to murder."

"I don't see no other way to get him to stop hurtin' people," Paul seethed, "People are losing everythin' because of him, even their lives."

"You can't prove he killed your father," Greenwood said. "Whoever did is best left alone. Your mother couldn't take another tragedy."

"Preacher," Paul sat up straighter, cocking his head toward the man beside him, his jaw tightening, "who said there would be another tragedy?"

"They killed your father and stole his savings. Who knows what else they'd do for these oil rights," suggested Greenwood, with a falsely apologetic smile.

I am the father of lies, and even I was impressed with the ease his falsehoods left his tongue. The air hung with a stiff silence, the two men not meeting each other's eyes. If truth is revealed by the mouth, it is found in the eyes.

"Maybe this is for the best, that your family leaves."

I'd gotten my hooks into Preacher Greenwood fairly early. People often see holy men as untouchable by my work, but if their spirit is weak and focused on earthly things, they too can be *swayed*.

Paul swallowed, "I never told you we lost our savings."

In Paul's heart, this might have been the greatest betrayal of Farewell. That the man who had sent his daddy off to Heaven with God's Word and a prayer had been on Mr. Washburn's payroll all along.

Nothing drives people further from God than crooked men of the cloth. Humans are incredibly stupid like that; always judging their Creator by the wickedness of their fellow man.

"How long?" Paul asked, breaking the deafening silence. "Clearly Mr. Washburn isn't paying you enough if you can't even fix up the church."

"Paul—"

"Was it at least worth more to you than my father's life," demanded Paul. Of course, Greenwood couldn't answer truthfully. Nothing on this earth was more valuable than a man's soul.

"You're too young to understand such things."

"Then help me understand, Preacher. And don't you dare put God's name in your mouth."

"You're one to talk about God's name while contemplating murder," Preacher Greenwood chastised maliciously. "Mr. Washburn does more for this town than you know. Because of him, people are staying in their homes, this church is still serving the community and people have work."

"At the cost of people being forced off their land and my father bein' killed."

"What proof do you have?"

"Sure, maybe I can't prove it but it don't mean it didn't happen that way," said Paul standing from the pew.

"Sit down!" Greenwood grabbed his shoulder, forcing the boy back on his ass, and stood himself. "You'd risk your soul and kill a man who could be innocent?"

Paul hesitated. All signs pointed to Washburn. He knew in his heart that if the banker hadn't pulled the trigger, he at least was the one who gave the order. But to make things interesting, there was one nudge I could give him, just to *really* test his resolve: doubt.

Doubt worms into the mind, creating indecisiveness and conflict. I'll admit I was disappointed in how quickly it took root in Paul. I had come to expect more from him, but I suppose he was finally wearing down. It was keeping him in his seat at least.

Preacher Greenwood stood, and began to pace near the pew, sensing the boy's hesitation, like a predator toying with its prey. "Your mother named you Paul, after Paul in the Bible, right?"

"Yes."

"She probably named you that so you'd be a learned man, a good writer. Right?"

"Yes."

"She named you well. You do take after Paul," Greenwood said, although perhaps not as a compliment. "He was zealous, too. But you know what the funny thing about Paul was?"

"No."

"As the Bible tells it, Paul was a Pharisee. He hated Christians, and took great joy in persecuting them, finding them and bringing them before the religious leaders."

"Yeah," Paul said, familiar enough with the story. "Then he went blind after seeing Christ and became a Christian when he could see again."

"Yes—" Mr. Greenwood paused his pacing, looking down at Paul, "—but before that, one of Jesus's followers, Stephen, was preaching the gospel. The Pharisees didn't like that, calling him a blasphemer. He was condemned by the Sanhedrin, then stoned to death."

Paul sat unmoving, listening to every word.

"Paul—then known as Saul— for all his fire and zeal, for all his hatred against the Christians, did not participate. Do you know what he did?"

Paul didn't answer. He knew.

"He held their coats," Preacher Greenwood said lightly. "For all your righteous indignation, you—like Saul—lack the conviction to get your hands *truly* dirty. You did nothing when Sheriff Fensky took a swing at you; you'll do nothing now as you lose your home."

Paul's jaw quivered slightly. Greenwood's harsh speech hurt worse than being beaten by a fist. Those bruises heal, but honest, cutting words did not. There was truth on Preacher Greenwood's filthy lips.

"Your family isn't wanted in Farewell or folks here would have tried to help you," Greenwood said. "This isn't your home anymore."

"I—"

"Get the hell out of my house, boy."

"Forgive me, Preacher," Paul stood up and reached for his hat. He stared at the Preacher, defeated in every way, but clinging to one last sliver of defiance, "I thought this was God's house, and that all were welcome."

Paul took leave of the church, his footsteps echoing darkly on the wood. Once he reached the stoop, he paused, kicked the dust from his boots, and carried on his way.

Chapter VI

Horrors and Horses

"WHAT are we going to do with all the furniture," Matty asked Paul, his eyes wandering around their empty shell of a home. All the sheets had been stripped off the mattresses and walls. The few photos they owned had also been taken down. All the food and silverware packed up. Even I, who loves despair, found the emptiness quite depressing.

It was delightful.

Paul knew they wouldn't be able to take everything with them to Sacramento. There wasn't a point to it anyway. It wasn't worth the effort to move rickety beds and an old table when his Aunt Geraldine wouldn't have space for such things.

The poor boy had been sullen all morning as he helped pack.

No, everything the Hopkins family would be taking with them sat packed in three battered suitcases and a carpet bag: clothes, the family Bible, and a few other personal items. Anna insisted on carrying Miss Maise herself, and Paul kept Isaiah's last letter safe in his pocket.

Mr. McGraw arrived at ten in the morning, rolling in on an old red pickup truck. He had been kind enough to offer them a ride to Worthingtown. No one else had and walking the ten miles would be a pain with Anna.

"I have errands to run anyway," he had said when he had stopped by to offer his help. "No trouble in giving you a lift."

Paul's heart dropped slightly, disappointed that Esther didn't come with. Looking at Mr. McGraw, it was obvious to see where

Esther got her looks. They shared the same strawberry hair and dimpled face.

Matty distracted himself from his sadness by following Mr. McGraw around, pestering him with incessant questions about engines and tires. He knew what an automobile was, but they weren't very common in Farewell. He'd certainly never had the chance to ride in one before.

Mr. McGraw was patient enough, but seemed all too eager to assist Gertrude as she came out of the house with the last suitcase, quickly taking it from her hands, "Allow me."

"Thank you."

Paul helped slide the luggage onto the truck bed, trying to sound casual, "Esther didn't wanna come?"

"She did, but she got scheduled at the bank and had to work," Mr. McGraw answered. "Why?"

"I was just hoping for a chance to say goodbye, is all."

"Well, you know where we live," Mr. McGraw said. "I'm sure she wouldn't mind you writing to her."

"You're right." Paul's spirit sank nonetheless. He and Esther didn't even get the chance to go on their date. It tore him apart that he never had that opportunity, and that was just fine with me. The more he looked back on the things he didn't get to do, the easier it would be to make him forget his future.

Gertrude did one last sweep around the house, checking all the nooks and crannies for anything they might have forgotten to pack, before wearily declaring, "Well, I think that's everything."

"Yeah, best get out of here before the sheriff shows up," Paul grumbled.

"Hush now, Paul," Gertrude scolded under her breath, handling everything with her usual stiff upper lip, "Mr. McGraw is being kind enough to give us a lift. I'll not have you complain."

"Yes Ma'am."

There was only enough room for two or three people in the cab of Mr. McGraw's truck. Gertrude was hesitant to let the children ride in the truck bed, but Mr. McGraw—much to Matty's excitement—assured her it was safe, so she allowed it.

Paul took Anna in his arms and lifted her playfully into the truck. She was dressed in her new flour sack dress, pink print and all. Without a doubt in Paul's mind, she'd be the prettiest little girl in all of Sacramento.

He stepped up on the wheel well and pulled himself onto the truck bed, sitting down with his legs dangling over the back.

Matty sat beside Paul and followed his brother's eyes back to their vacant farmhouse. It would probably be gone by the end of the week, like their existence didn't matter. Paul thought that it didn't feel right to leave. That perhaps someone should say a few words to mark the occasion, like a funeral.

Humans are like that. They cling to rituals to try to find significance in the insignificant. They act like such things matter in the long term, as if giving meaning to something will make it hurt less when it is gone.

Such thoughts attract me like a moth to a flame. Of course, nothing matters in this stupid, ugly world. It's a lovely paradigm that children are the most susceptible to heartbreak and upset, yet are the ones most powerless to stop it.

Mr. McGraw started the truck and drove off.

The small farmhouse grew smaller and smaller until it faded from view, like an insignificant speck on an unbroken horizon.

❧ ❧ ❧ ❧ ❧

They didn't say much on the ride to Worthingtown. Gertrude tried to make polite small talk with Mr. McGraw, but after about fifteen minutes they let the sounds of the jolting truck and wind fill the silence.

Driving to Worthingtown didn't take long anyway.

The town was only slightly larger than Farewell, but it was twice as lively and half as drab. The buildings weren't nearly as decrepit; some even had fresh paint. It didn't have the alluring, oppressive feel of hopelessness I enjoyed and had become accustomed to.

"You mind if I make a few stops before I drop you off, Mrs. Hopkins? Just a couple of errands," Mr. McGraw asked as he navigated through the town slowly and carefully.

Matty started to complain about having to go on errands, but Gertrude hushed him up quickly and he became almost as sullen as his brother. I could tell that in a few bad years, Matthew would end up the spitting image of Paul.

"We don't mind," Gertrude said. "Our train doesn't leave for a while."

I had planted the seed in Mr. McGraw's head that he should run errands today, and kill two birds with one stone. He is a busy man, and he needed things in Worthingtown anyway. Not to mention that it was his truck and his generosity. The Hopkins could stand to wait after he had been so nice as to drive them.

"I just gotta buy feed," Mr McGraw said, pointing up the road towards the general store, "and stop by the post office." He gestured just a bit further up.

Matty muttered something about having a post office in Farewell. Paul jabbed him lightly in the ribs to shut him up. They already caused their mother enough grief today.

The truck shuddered to a halt outside the general store. Gertrude turned to face her children, clutching her handbag, "I'm going to go in with Mr. McGraw and get a few things for the train. Behave, and don't go anywhere."

"Yes ma'am."

Immediately after Gertrude was in the store and out of earshot, Matty poked Anna.

"Ow!"

"Leave her alone, Matty."

"You're not Pa," he said sourly.

Paul resisted the urge to smack his little brother upside the head, which would have been rather amusing for me. I love it when children fight. Matty, however, decided not to provoke his siblings further. Shameful, but never mind that. Things would get far more interesting to me in due time.

Paul quietly watched people go about their day. A man tied up a white mare alongside some other horses before heading into a saloon. Two ladies walked along arm in arm, one laughing at what the other said. He pointed out their pretty dresses to Anna so she could admire the ruffles and colors the women wore.

"Look at that purple dress, Anna, ain't— *isn't* that pretty?" he asked, correcting himself as Anna climbed onto his lap with Miss Maise.

"Mama said that's lavender."

"It's purple enough."

"Lavender!"

"Fine, it's lavender," Paul conceded. "Well, I spy, with my little eye, something . . . blue."

"The sky!" Anna guessed.

"No, good try though. Matty?" asked Paul. It was a pointless, stupid game. He was only trying to keep the little ones occupied and their minds off their troubles.

Matty rolled his eyes. "The general store sign."

"Okay, your turn."

"I spy with my little eye . . . something," Matty looked around the street for a few moments, "Something red."

Anna pointed at a hawkish woman. "The lady's hat!"

"Don't point. It's not nice," Paul scolded. "Was it the hat?"

Matty shook his head. Anna and Paul tried again, searching for red. Ever the good brother, Paul subtly gestured to the item so Anna would win.

"The bucket!"

"Good job! Okay, now it's your turn," Paul said with forced enthusiasm.

"Yellow!"

"Something yellow?" Matty asked. There was very little yellow to be seen, even less so than the red and blue in a dreary place like this. Paul and Matty tried asking for hints, looking up and down the street.

That's when Paul—the oblivious idiot he was—finally saw the Mineral and Oil Land Office sign nailed to a red building. Lace curtains hung in the windows and a large yellow bench decorated the wide stoop.

Took him long enough.

Isaiah's last letter grew heavy in Paul's pocket, weighing him down on one side like an unbalanced scale. In the next couple of hours he'd be on a train to California and never have this chance again. Then again, he thought, maybe he shouldn't.

But anything unbalanced always tips to one side.

"Matty, watch Anna," Paul instructed.

"But Mama said—"

"I said to watch Anna!"

He'd be back before Ma even knew he was gone, he told himself, wading out into the kicked-up street dust. He couldn't go to California without knowing the truth of it all. It would only take a minute to get peace of mind.

I love the lies people tell themselves. Who am I to stop it? In the end, it wouldn't matter if Paul began to tell himself the truth to himself now; I win either way.

"Excuse me, ma'am," Paul said, brushing past the same woman in lavender that he pointed out to Anna. He glanced back just to make sure he could see the truck from the office. Sure enough, Matty and Anna were still there.

The Mineral and Oil Land Office had a bright and cheery interior, with those lace curtains hanging over floral chintz seats placed in a waiting area, giving colorful contrast to the whitewashed walls. A plump, middle-aged woman sat at a desk across from the door.

She smiled, "Can I help you, young man?"

"Yes, ma'am," Paul suddenly remembered to remove his hat, still reeling from his sudden impulsiveness, "I'm lookin' for a Mr. Lorry."

"You have an appointment?"

"No, ma'am."

"Name?"

"Mr. Paul Hopkins."

The woman pointed vaguely to one of the spare chairs, "Take a seat, and I'll see if he has a second."

"Thank you, Ma'am."

By the time Paul got himself comfortable in the rather uncomfortable chairs, his name was already being called by a fat man in a bright plaid shirt. "You must be Mr. Lorry," he said.

Mr. Lorry returned Paul's handshake cordially, "Hopkins, huh? You must be Isaiah's son."

"Yes, sir."

Mr. Lorry blanched. Isaiah had been a good friend of his and it wounded him in all the ways I love to see man hurt, but men aren't liable to display such weakness.

"I'm very sorry to hear about your father. I wanted to come to the funeral—"

"Do you have a minute to talk?" Paul interrupted. It might have been rude, but the last thing he wanted was to hear more useless platitudes.

"Of course," Mr. Lorry gave a thin smile, almost apologetic. "Come on, let's go to my office."

Paul remained silent as he followed Lorry deeper into the office, and into a small room that was rather bare, save for the desk crowded with papers, and two wooden chairs.

Mr. Lorry took a seat, "What can I do for you, Paul?"

"I am here about the survey," Paul said. He pulled out the papers Esther had given him. "My father thought there was oil on the land and he named you his business partner."

"He said he was gonna do that. Your father and I were friends, went to school together."

"You did?"

"Yeah. It's why Isaiah came to me about the survey, thinking there would be oil. He knew I worked at the Land Office and wanted to keep things discreet."

"What made him think there was oil?"

"Isaiah discovered sandstone formations across your property. It was nothing significant, but he knew there was a chance it might mean oil and reached out to me to survey the area." Lorry stood up and walked over to an oak cabinet, flipping through a stack of documents before pulling out a folder.

"He never came back for the results. I thought he was just having trouble coming up with the money, so I held onto them until he came back . . . then I heard he'd died." He handed Paul the folder. "Here, you're welcome to take a look. They're yours now."

Paul opened the folder hungrily, flipping through pages of data he didn't understand. The tables and charts meant nothing to him. He searched desperately for something recognizable.

"I think this is the reason he was killed. His papers were found in Mr. Washburn's office," Paul looked up for a moment to gauge Mr. Lorry's reaction. He didn't know if this man was familiar with the banker.

Mr. Lorry's sigh was all the confirmation he needed, "Isaiah told me how close he was to paying back the loan. I knew if Washburn found out about any oil, the farm was at risk since he put it up for collateral. It was actually me who suggested he move his savings here to Worthingtown's bank."

"Do you really think Mr. Washburn would have . . . '' Paul started.

"Have you ever heard about what happened to the Osage?" Mr. Lorry asked, gently interrupting Paul.

"No."

Mr. Lorry sighed, "The Osage Indians were forced off their land into a reservation in Oklahoma. About ten years ago, they became some of the richest people in the world. Long story short, they found oil. The Osage profited from it and lived like damn royalty."

Mr. Lorry's tone turned dark. Paul listened even more intently, looking up from the survey results in his hand.

"The share each Osage got from the oil was called a headright and when that Indian died, the money would be paid to their next of kin or heir. The catch is, that a white man could inherit a headright in the right circumstances. So white folk married into these Osage families, and the Osage started dropping like flies."

"What?"

"Over thirty people were murdered, even a house bombed. Finally, the federal government got involved to try to solve the case. All those Indians dead for what? Money?

"Shortly after all that, Ned Washburn moved from Osage County and opened a bank," Mr. Lorry leaned forward in his chair conspiratorially. "Where'd you think he got the money to do that?"

"He killed for it?"

"Killing for inheritance?" Mr. Lorry laughed dryly, clapping a hand to his knee. "It's the oldest trick in the book other than murder itself. Dunno how the bastard got away with it, just that he left the county rich enough to open a bank."

"You're certain?"

"No. I can't prove anything. Only conjecture."

"I know we lost the farm, but is there a way the oil could help us?" Paul asked. "Or prove what Mr. Washburn did?"

Mr. Lorry sighed once more, almost painfully.

Paul's heart skipped a beat, flipping to the final page in the file, "What?"

"There's no oil on that land."

"You have to be lying." Paul's first thought was that Mr. Washburn had paid off Mr. Lorry like everyone else, but he read the survey again and there it was, official as could be. There was no oil.

"I walked the land with your father at least half a dozen times," Lorry said apologetically. "Your farm doesn't have oil on it. Certainly not enough to warrant a dig. I'm sorry. Truly."

People have this weird notion that if they don't consider the possibility of the worst happening, the worst won't happen. Humans live so easily in denial that they are safe, or that nothing can hurt them. The universe would *never* be so unfair as to take away the one thing they are desperately clinging to. Paul was clinging to that oil because if it wasn't there, it meant his daddy died for nothing.

His daddy died for nothing.

Paul placidly stood from his chair, "Thank you for your time. Sorry to have bothered you."

"Now son, I understand if you might need a minute, perhaps a brandy—" Mr. Lorry offered kindly.

"I left my siblings in the truck," Paul mumbled numbly. "I should be getting back to them."

"Well, don't be afraid to contact us if you need anything," Mr. Lorry said hesitantly.

Humans are wickedly intelligent, always striving, learning, and creating. Yet when they are faced with someone who has experienced loss, they can never find the right thing to say. Mr. Lorry was no exception to this. Not that anything he could have said would prevent what was to come.

Young Paul left the office with nothing more than a few niceties and a half-assed offer of support that came too late.

Now, this is where it gets *fun*.

Once outside, Paul doubled over as gracefully as a newborn foal. He rested against the wall of the Land Office, with his hands on his knees, coming to grips with what he had just discovered. The conversation had left his mouth drier than the desert, and his muscles weak. That weakness took hold for only a moment before it gave way to strength and rage, like dying coals sparking into an inferno.

Children are so insistent that the world is a fair and just place. There are few things more fascinating—or fun—than their reaction when they are confronted with the truth that the world is anything but.

I love when there is no way for Justice to prevail. Justice can so easily be blurred with Revenge, and Revenge prevails where Justice does not. It's easy to justify the murder of an evil man.

The sky itself seemed to darken as Paul collected what he could of himself and walked the street once more. He barely registered anything other than a single thought driving him forward, repeating over and over like a broken record.

His daddy had died for nothing.

Matty and Anna were still alone in the truck, meaning the adults were still wasting time in the store. Good. It would make things less complicated for Paul.

"Paul, where did ya go?" Matty asked as his brother opened the truck door.

"I had to talk to someone," Paul answered shortly. He rifled through the cab, getting straight to his dirty business. "Where's the rifle?"

"What?"

"Where's the rifle, Matty?" Paul snapped.

"Up front under the seat. Why?"

Paul retrieved the gun, slinging it over his back, and turned to leave. On second thought, he grasped Matty's shoulder, his calico shirt crumpling underneath his fingers. Paul met his brother's eyes with an intense gaze, "Take care of Ma and Anna, alright?"

Matty gulped, "Where are you going?"

"I left something back at home," Paul lied. In his mind, there was no use in scaring his siblings, "I'll be right back."

"You'll miss the train!"

"Paul, don't go!" Anna wailed.

"I'll be fine, just . . . I love you, okay? Tell Ma I love her, too," Paul said in a hard voice, kissing his sister's forehead. "Be good, Anna."

I do love it when a person's resolve sets in, like steel taking shape. After that, only the fire consuming them can hope to weaken their mettle.

Paul turned his back on his siblings, marching down the road to hell.

What do people say, that the road to hell is paved with good intentions? I can assuredly say most of the time it's not. It's paved with the bones of men who were proud enough to think their intentions were good. The bones of men who think nothing of stealing a horse because murder is in their heart.

Paul had never stolen before in his life. His daddy would have whipped him for such stupidity. There were so many horses tethered outside the shops that it wasn't difficult to approach the white mare that was already saddled and untie her as though she belonged to him. He hooked his foot on the stirrup and swung himself up onto her back, for once looking like the white knight he always made himself out to be.

It's fitting. In the game of chess, knights are an invaluable piece, moving across the board in unorthodox ways, able to jump and surpass other pieces in ways not even a queen can. They are best utilized when surrounded by enemy pieces.

If Isaiah's death was my opening move, then I do believe we are nearing checkmate.

With a snap of the reins—and the uproar of nearby townsfolk—Paul was off, galloping down the road out of Worthingtown kicking up a trail of dust in his wake.

Chapter VII

Damnation and Death

THEY say death rides in on a white horse.

Paul snapped the reins, urging the mare forward the whole ten miles back to Farewell.

Men have free will. I can convince them to do nothing unless they assent, but in their fallen nature it is entirely too easy to tempt them to sin. All you have to do is be loud and drown out all other recourse until all they hear is the path to condemnation calling them.

What Paul was about to do, he did of his own free will. I just . . . *aided* him along where I could.

The people of Farewell never should have ignored the Hopkins family in their suffering. Very soon they were going to have to raise their heads and witness the cost of their negligence, but none of them would claim responsibility for it.

Gill saw Paul riding by from the window of the saloon as he wiped down tables in preparation for customers. By the end of the day, the whole bar would be filled with men gossiping like fishwives, and Gill would be having his most profitable night in months.

Mr. Jefferies, the grocer, would be there, recounting how he too saw young Paul Hopkins racing through town on a horse he didn't own. Gill would pour him another drink and ask the patrons what they knew of the boy.

The town would talk all night but in the present moment, Paul was becoming a man of *action*.

Paul pulled hard on the reins, the mare halting just a short distance from the bank, kicking up another billowing cloud of dust. I might as well have waltzed on it, dancing to the tune of hastily acted-upon anger and the beat of Paul's pounding heart.

The boy dismounted the weary mare, reaching behind him for the comforting presence of the rifle in his hands. His father had taught him how to shoot, after all. Maybe, just maybe, Paul prayed, he would have his father's blessing in this.

You never point the barrel of this gun at something you don't want shot. So be damned sure when you aim this thing, you want what's in front of you full of lead.

Those were Isaiah's words. A good son obeys his father.

Paul Hopkins calmly and quietly stepped into the bank, a gust of wind trailing behind him. Nearly a dozen souls inside stared back at him as his footsteps echoed across the wood floor, watching the rifle in his hands. An older man at the counter reached to his waist for a revolver that wasn't there. Two mothers held fast to their children, cowering away. One of them even shrieked as her eyes landed on his weapon.

Paul swallowed hard, ignoring the fear in their eyes. They assumed he was there to rob the bank and further send them into ruin. Paul had no such intentions, but he let them think what they wanted. Their fear would keep them out of his way.

He searched the space until his gaze found familiar strawberry-blonde curls and the prettiest face he ever did see.

Paul went to Esther. She was the only one in the bank he could trust. Unlike the others, she was looking at *him* rather than the gun.

"Where is he?" Paul asked quietly, his knuckles whitening around the grip of the rifle.

"Paul—" She breathed.

"Esther, please . . . ''

Remember when I said that Esther McGraw would be Ned's undoing? If he had treated her right, she might not have consigned him to his fate. She recognized the look in Paul's eyes. She knew what he was about to do.

"He's upstairs," Esther whispered. "In his office still."

Paul left the counter and headed up the narrow wooden staircase, each step carrying him further away from the possibility of a long life with Esther McGraw.

In another life, or another time, Paul might've stolen a kiss and told her how he felt. He would have swept her up in his arms and danced for hours, promising her all the fine things in the world she deserved.

In another time, Esther would have given him that kiss so he needn't steal it.

I have no interest in the musings of happily ever after. That's not why I'm here. The world is cruel and cold, and people like Paul and Esther don't get to hope for what they will never have.

Paul didn't have the politeness to knock on Ned's office door, or the audacity to kick it down. He was beyond such immaturity. He entered with a twist of a doorknob and the creak of unoiled hinges.

The office itself was rather plain. The nicest thing Paul was able to take stock of was a clock on the wall, ticking down the seconds one by one. Books, dusty with disuse, lined a small shelf. And sitting at a desk, littered with paperwork and ashtrays, was Ned Washburn.

He looked up from his work long enough to acknowledge Paul, before turning back to the papers, unbothered. "So, Mr. Hopkins, how can I help you? Before Sheriff Fensky arrives, of course."

Blood rushed to Paul's ears as the sinful anger crept around him like a cocoon.

"I just want the truth."

"Oh? About what?"

Paul could barely force out the words. He never considered that learning the truth might be harder than staying forever in limbo, but he made himself ask. His father deserved that much.

"Where were you on July eighth?"

"Probably working," Ned answered, keeping his tone a tad incredulous. It was condescending as all hell, and so I encouraged it. Anything to break down young Paul.

"Did you know my father was closing out his account here?"

"No."

"You're a damned liar, Mr. Washburn," Paul said softly.

"Easy there now, son—"

"Don't call me son," Paul threatened in a cold voice. Ned didn't have the right to claim anything paternal over him.

"Alright," Ned said placatingly, still sitting calmly at his desk and unbothered by the vengeful boy. "Listen, just put the gun down ... ''

"Did you know he was looking for oil on our property?"

"I had some suspicions, but nothing came of it. There's no oil on your farm, son," Ned said. He reached into his desk, and Paul gripped his gun ever tighter, but Ned only pulled out two glasses and a bottle of cognac. He poured the drink before sliding one over to Paul. The boy needed no drink to steady his nerves. Not for this.

"Did you find that out before or after you had my father killed?"

The office filled with uproarious laughter. Ned doubled over as if Paul had said nothing more than a good joke. "Is that why you break into my bank with a gun and threaten me in my office? Because you think I killed your father?"

"Go ahead," Paul seethed. It was funny watching his anger be dismissed by Ned. "Deny it."

"I think the Sheriff had a working theory that your father was taking your family's money and leaving town since he wasn't gonna be able to take care of y'all," Ned said casually, hoping his light-hearted demeanor would provoke the boy. He just had to make Paul look insane. Unreasonable. Ned downed his drink, "Shame he got robbed."

"You killed him, just admit it! Admit you killed my father, and threatened Esther, and cheated your way into owning our land."

"My land, son—"

"I said don't—"

"*My* land. . . . It legally belongs to me now. Not even the oil could have saved your farm, and your father was an idiot for thinking he could try to best me."

"Who pulled the trigger?" Paul demanded.

"You wouldn't know him. Just a stranger desperate for cash. I can't even remember his name as we spoke only twice."

"Where can I find him?"

Ned gave Paul a patronizing look. Instantly, the boy knew the man was dead, probably killed by Sheriff Fensky. Ned handled these things meticulously, after all. Moves and countermoves. Just like chess.

Paul wrinkled his nose, "No loose ends, right?"

"I wonder how many loose ends you'll leave behind," Ned started, malicious as ever, "Your mother?"

"Don't—"

"Your siblings . . . Ms. McGraw."

"Stop!"

Ned smiled darkly, like a leech latching onto Paul's weakness, his love for others. Everyone had something he could use to control them. "They all knew you came here with a gun. I daresay Esther even helped you up here. Shame if the sheriff found *that* out."

"Leave 'er out of this," Paul warned. "I made 'er tell me."

"You'll be ruining a lot of people if you shoot me."

"I don't wanna kill you, Mr. Washburn," Paul said quietly, jabbing the barrel of the gun in Washburn's direction. "Get moving. We're going to Worthingtown."

Ned seemed a bit surprised at this announcement, and once more he regarded Paul with piqued curiosity. "Worthingtown?"

"You're gonna confess you had my father killed," Paul said, more to himself than the other man. He desperately believed that he could make this right. "You're gonna go to prison."

"With what proof? You came in here with a gun. Could have forced me to say anything."

"We have the papers."

"Circumstantial at best," Ned taunted. "You'd be unable to prove anything, certainly now that the trigger man is dead."

"I'll testify."

Ned chortled darkly, "And who would corroborate your story? I'll confess happily, but I doubt I'll go to prison. After all, I'm speaking to you under duress. You have the gun."

He was right. Everyone had been right, down to the corrupt preacher. No one in Farewell would have the courage to speak against Mr. Washburn. There was nothing Paul could do.

You are dust and to dust you will return.

Ned sat back down at his desk, leaning in his chair. "Put the gun away. We both know you don't have it in you, son—"

He died instantly from the bullet Paul put between his eyes.

The banker fell forward and slumped over his desk, the blood soaking into the wood and papers underneath.

I laughed heartily. My time in Farewell hadn't gone to waste.

Paul Hopkins had not disappointed me. Not even now as he stepped back away from Ned's corpse, gulping air into his lungs as fast as it left him, steadying himself as he lowered the rifle.

Paul couldn't quite tear himself away from the sight. Forcing himself to look while he searched for some remorse in his soul, but found, of all things, that he wasn't sorry. Ned Washburn had ruined too many lives without consequence, and without feeling remorse.

I wrapped my arms around Paul and his soul. I certainly couldn't worm my way in right now, but the opportunity was there. All I had to do was convince him there was no redemption from this.

Yelling and commotion sounded from downstairs. Paul had expected the sheriff and his deputies would come for him. He set aside the rifle, resigned—to my great disappointment. In my opinion, if you commit murder once, what's taking one more life? Still, the boy was young and the path ahead of him was shrouded.

I could be patient.

Sheriff Fensky rushed into the office, colt drawn, leveling it at Paul's chest. The veins in his neck bulged dangerously close to bursting.

"Hands where I can see them!"

Paul raised his hands.

"Dear God, have mercy," Fensky's attention fell on the dead man in the room rather than the living. His face fell a bit, seeing his friend with a hole in his skull. It was rather self-righteous of him to act in such a way, considering the blood he had spilt.

"What happened, boy?"

"I shot him."

"Really?" Fensky asked, suspicious that the boy would give himself up so easily. "The McGraw girl down there said Ned shot himself."

"I know what I done Sheriff," Paul said plainly, "and I ain't gonna apologize for it, neither."

Sheriff Fensky scowled, walking around behind Paul before wrenching his arms down painfully, purposefully cruel as he cinched on the handcuffs. "You're a sick son of a bitch, Hopkins."

Was Fensky right, Paul wondered. He glanced back at the body lying over the desk, and just for a moment Ned's corpse reminded him of Mr. Kinley. A sick son of bitch, he might be, but the one thing he'd concede having in common with Ned was a lack of remorse. All was settled in his heart, mind, and soul.

Sheriff Fensky roughly grabbed Paul's arm, shoving him forward through the door while snapping at a deputy to cover up the body. As if that would make this go away.

It would not. This wound would fester in Farewell for quite some time. For years, they would gossip and debate—most of it speculation—whether Paul Hopkins had been insane or a hero. A madman or a martyr.

What remained an unequivocal fact was that when Sheriff Fensky marched downstairs and demanded the bank patrons give statements on what they witnessed, not a single person in Farewell would raise their voice against Paul.

I won't share with you much more. All you need to know is that I am satisfied with how things played out. It ended in death and the people of Farewell rejoiced in that death. Rejoicing in a man's death, even an evil one, is indeed a wicked, *wicked* thing. So Farewell remains my little kingdom where I can twist and manipulate men into wretched, sinful things.

Now, this story may be about Paul Hopkins, but you might ask who *I* am, or how I know so intimately the details of what was in that boy's heart when he pulled that fateful trigger?

I'm just the Devil that made him do it.

ABOUT THE AUTHOR

Lavinia Love was born in Minnesota and graduated from college in Duluth. She has been writing professionally for several years. She enjoys going to Mass, game nights with friends, nautical and nuclear, and canola fields.

She currently lives in a plains state with the love of her life, and has a contentious relationship with her pet cat. Lavinia can be contacted on Tumblr at the blog *live-laugh-lavinialove*.

You can read Lavinia's stories, get updates, ask questions, leave comments and more at her website:

https://livelaughlavinialove.wixsite.com/writing

SWORD OF DOMINIC PRESS

Sword of Dominic Press is a Christian writing organization dedicated to helping independent writers bring their projects to publication. Here, you'll find devout Christian writers from all walks of life, writing stories across a variety of genres, including alternative fiction, space westerns, fantasy, horror, and more. Also available is a team of freelance editors, beta-readers, and designers to make the publication process easier.

Our mission is to bring quality ideas and stories, rooted in Christian values, to a wide audience.

See what we're all about on Tumblr (*swordofdominic*) and our website:

https://swordofdominic.wixsite.com/sodp